Plenty of Fish

in the Ocean State

Mary Walsh

Stephanie —

From my bookshelf

to yours!

Mary Walsh

Discover other books by Mary Walsh

Once Upon a Time in Chicago
His Second Chance
Wounded but not Dead
Fine Spirits Served Here
You Deserve Better
Where or When
Life Lessons for My Kids
Stable of Studs
Dragon Slayer
Catch a Break

Plenty of Fish in the Ocean State

Copyright © 2021
Published by Mary Walsh

For Niki
My soul sister
You are the ying to my yang

CHAPTER 1

I awoke to the sound of my TV downstairs, murmuring sounds like Charlie Brown's schoolteacher. I must have left it on last night when I went to bed. The girls and I had a great time last night at Wickenden Pub. Ebony, Jenna, and Valeria--Val for short--joined me at our favorite dive bar. I drew the short straw as the designated driver. My name is Reese--yes, like the peanut butter cup--and I live in Providence, Rhode Island.

As I dragged myself out of bed to start a crisp August Saturday morning, my head throbbed. But why? I didn't have any alcohol. I was sure of it. Val and Jenna downed the local favorite lager, Narragansett, while

Ebony stuck to her usual drink, Buffalo Trace Bourbon. Neat, because she's cool like that. I had some seltzer and a lime--something more appealing than plain water so the barmaid didn't give me the stink eye for wasting her time. If I only had seltzer last night, why did my head hurt like I won a shot drinking contest? Which I had done a year after I graduated from Villanova, but that's a story for another day.

I dropped back down on my bed and massaged my throbbing temples. This was not going to be a good day if I couldn't even get out of bed.

A *clomp clomp clomp* of feet shuffling on the first floor echoed from my kitchen. The sound traveled up the stairs and down the hallway to my bedroom. My shaking fingers curled around my blanket in fear.

Someone was downstairs in my house! My menacing headache immediately transformed to a Category 1 hurricane while I frantically searched for my phone. It wasn't on my dresser where I normally put it when I went to bed. As I burrowed through my pillows and covers like a groundhog, my heart raced. Where was my freaking phone? I needed to call 911!

Clomp clomp clomp again.

I gasped, standing perfectly still willing the intruder not to come into my bedroom. But I couldn't stay cornered in my bedroom. Jumping out the bedroom window would result in a few broken bones. I weighed my options carefully and decided to take action. Snatching a wire hairbrush from my dresser, I clutched it close to my chest and slowly opened my bedroom door. The intruder was in for a fight.

As I tip-toed down the hall, a squeaky floorboard betrayed my stealth mode. I froze and held my breath. When I didn't hear anyone coming up the steps, I continued on soft feet. As I approached the top of the stairs, I considered my choices. I could gradually descend and hope that I didn't encounter any more squeaky floorboards, or bolt down. But I needed some extra time to plan my attack. I opted for the former. The burglar could be six-foot-eight and weigh 300 pounds. At five-foot-three and 123 pounds, I'd be a bantamweight fighter up against a heavyweight. Someone like that could easily lift me and toss me around. Having run track in high school, I could dart out of the house but wasn't sure how far I'd get in bare feet.

Why was someone in my house on a Saturday morning anyway? To steal my dust-filled waffle iron?

7

Have at it. I had never felt scared about being a single woman living alone in an old house. Until now.

After I crept down the stairs without making a sound, I reached the bottom and exhaled. More shuffling sounds came from my kitchen. A cabinet opened and closed. Dishes clanged together. What the hell? Take everything you want, just get out of my house!

As I squeezed the hairbrush in my white-knuckled fingers, I inched my way through the living room. Saturday morning news blared on the TV. The intruder was watching the news and pillaging my kitchen? What kind of burglar was this?

Hiding at the entrance to my kitchen, I studied my surroundings to plan my attack. Unfortunately, I could only see one side of the room and the intruder was out of my line of sight. He or she was in the blind corner, where the fridge was. Was the intruder now stealing my eggs?

I spied my phone on the counter a few steps in front of me. Why did I leave it downstairs? If I could get the phone without making a sound, I could call 911 and the police could do their thing. They would arrest a news-watching, waffle-iron-and-egg-stealing burglar. The intruder would be a laughingstock at the Providence

8

City Jail, but at least the trespasser would be out of my house.

I took one step, paused, and stared at the intruder who was now looting my fridge. His back to me, he was undressed from the waist up and had bare feet. His toned, mocha skin dipped into a pair of black shorts, but I couldn't see his face. His ass could cloud a girl's thoughts. Confused by his appearance, I couldn't take another step. At least I had found the intruder and he seemed harmless. My heart rate slowed.

Who was this twin-of-Adonis man in my kitchen? And why was he taking food out of my fridge? He didn't act like a dangerous intruder. Maybe he was lost? From the back, he seemed familiar, but I was still hesitant to make myself known. My headache prevented me from focusing. Slowly, I lowered my hairbrush and cocked my head to the side. I didn't pick up a guy at Wickenden Pub and bring him home last night. I was sure of it.

Suddenly, the man turned around and grinned at me with a blazing white smile. My initial fear turned to awe. Tension left my body in an instant.

"'Morning, Reese. I was wondering when you were getting up."

Mateo.

We had dated for a few months a year ago, and I liked his lifestyle, but I never felt a real love connection with him -- at least not emotionally. Though our physical chemistry could cause a forest fire. He was a hottie with a body thanks to his job as a personal trainer. When I had needed an ego boost in the past year, I texted him for a hookup. Our naked bodies garnered a great workout every month or so. But I didn't remember doing that last night. Why was he here?

I remained still for an extra second, not wishing to interrupt the surreal moment.

"Want an omelet for breakfast? I'm making one for myself." He held a few of my eggs in his hand. Oh, those magical fingers could make my heart race when we were in bed.

"Um... I..." was all I could utter and fumbled placing the hairbrush on the counter. All of a sudden, I forgot that I thought he was an intruder.

"I couldn't find any tomatoes. Do you want onions and peppers?" Mateo stood in front of the open fridge and smirked at me, his shorts struggling to stay up on his toned hips.

I gaped at him, still stunned that he was in my kitchen...and that he was barely dressed. My mind

10

wandered to hot memories of us testing out the springs in my bed a month ago. I nodded, silently picking up my hairbrush again and pulling it through my hair.

"I can make some bacon too if you have it," he said, rooting through my half-empty fridge.

"In the drawer," I muttered and pointed with my hairbrush.

"What's with the brush?" he asked. His dark hair was perfectly swept up into a small, wavy pompadour. Did he never get bedhead?

"Um… I…" I rocked the brush back and forth in my hand. Realizing how dumb my attack plan was, I set it on the counter. "Never mind."

Mateo turned back into the fridge and grabbed a package of bacon and some shredded cheese out of the drawer. Making himself comfortable in my kitchen, he shut the fridge and carried the provisions to a counter near the stove. Next, he grabbed an onion and pepper from a nearby plate of fresh vegetables that I had picked from my garden a few days earlier. He didn't have any tomatoes because I had given my extras to the girls last night. More would be coming in a few days.

"I made some coffee, too," Mateo said as he heated a pan on the stove and opened the bacon. The

11

bacon sizzled as he laid it on the griddle. As the salty aroma filled the air, my stomach lurched in response. As much as I loved bacon, it wasn't a welcome sight. My body might mutiny if I tried to eat it.

"What-- What are you doing here? How did you get in?" I was finally able to utter a full sentence. My headache flared again, now that my adrenaline had subsided.

"You asked me to come over last night," Mateo answered as he chopped peppers and onions on a cutting board. "Don't you remember?"

"I did?"

"Yeah, around midnight." He winked at me then found another pan from the cabinet and heated it. "Maybe I'm losing my touch since you don't remember."

I quickly ran through the events of last night in my head. Val, Ebony, Jenna, and I left the bar around 11:00. Ebony had a breakfast meeting this morning so we didn't stay out late like we normally do. I dropped off all three of them within fifteen minutes and was home by 11:20. As far as I remembered, I immediately went to bed.

"Did we...?" I pointed a finger back and forth between him and me.

"Have sex?" Mateo turned to face me, a spatula in his hand. He jumped back as a rogue drop of bacon grease bounced from the pan and headed for his smooth tawny chest. "No."

The first time Mateo and I had sex a year ago, I stumbled like a newborn giraffe for two days. We had met on Tinder and the rumors proved true--it was a hookup site. That night he had thrown me up against a headboard and I discovered I liked being manhandled. A couple of days later, I found a faint bruise on my tailbone from the fun. The fallout was worth it.

"Why not?" I asked. If Mateo wasn't at my house for a booty call, then why was he there?

"Because you fell asleep and I don't do unconscious. I slept on your couch." He turned back to the pan and combined everything like a wizard conjuring a spell. "Coulda been a fun night, but you were out cold."

I smirked at the idea of a hot and sweaty night between us but things still weren't making sense to me.

"Can you grab a couple of plates and forks while I finish this up?" Mateo asked. He flipped the bacon.

"Sure." I stretched up and pulled two plates from the overhead cabinet and two forks from the drawer and set them on the counter next to Mateo.

"Breakfast is served." Mateo slid a fluffy omelet onto a plate, placed a few pieces of bacon on it, and handed it to me. He did the same for himself. After nights of ravaging me in my bed, Mateo often rewarded me with breakfast the next morning. Eggs were his specialty. But now, I wasn't sure if I could manage a bite.

"Thank you. You're so sweet to do this. Mornings with you are almost as fun as the night before."

"Thanks. I always have fun with you too."

Mateo joined me at my kitchen table. He and I became comfortable with each other over the past year and I didn't mind him in my house. He was good company when I wasn't out with the girls.

In between bites, I rubbed my temples, trying to get rid of the headache.

"You okay?" Mateo asked.

"I don't know. I haven't had a bad headache like this in forever." I chased the eggs around the plate with my fork.

"Did you get smashed last night?"

"No, I was the DD. I only had seltzer." I silently begged him to help me find an answer.

"You forgot texting me and you have a bad headache. You sure you didn't get roofied?" Mateo pointed at me with his fork.

"I don't think so. The girls and I were at our own table the whole night. Some guys came by to talk, but nobody was near my drink. I'm sure of it."

"Maybe you should take it easy today." Mateo took a bite of his omelet.

"I plan on it."

"I gotta head to the gym soon, but I can check on you later." Mateo rested his hand on my wrist.

"Thanks. I appreciate it." I kissed him on the cheek. "You're sweet."

The doorbell rang, interrupting us. Now what? Who was coming to my house on a Saturday morning? With all this traffic, my house was becoming a Dunkin' Donuts drive-thru.

15

CHAPTER 2

Leaving Mateo in the kitchen, I found an abandoned sweatshirt on my couch and tossed it over top of my sleep tank and shorts. Can't look like a hot mess. Don't want to scare the neighbors. I lived on a quiet block where the most exciting news was when tomatoes ripened.

Two years ago, I bought the 1920s bungalow on Ingraham Street in East Providence. Owning a century-old home had its challenges with moody wiring, questionable plumbing, and single-pane windows that had never been replaced. New England winters forced me to wear a parka to bed. A previous owner had painted the original cedar clapboard shingles and now the outside of my house was mint green. Right after I moved in, I single-handedly removed all of the 1980s wallpaper and painted all of the rooms. I had yet to build a deck on the back. I might have to enlist Mateo's help for that. The location made me happy that I could walk a couple of blocks in any direction and get pizza at PieZoni's, a pastry fix at Morningstar Bakery, or Thai street food. A Del's Lemonade truck was parked up the street serving cool, sweet drinks for summertime fans.

I opened the front door to a familiar face.

Luke.

"I just read your text and brought you some breakfast." He held a brown paper bag and a to-go cup in his hands. "Iced coffee and a muffin."

Luke and I were set up on a blind date six months earlier by my next-door neighbor, Mrs. Patterson. She kept badgering me to set me up with her friend's grandson and I finally caved. Luke could pass for a tall D'Artagnan's doppelganger with a headful of shaggy blonde hair and a soul patch goatee. Perfect for his laid-back job as a boat wrapper. He was the best in the business and had a long list of clients along the coast who wanted him to prep their boats for the winter. If I ever wanted to rent a boat at the marina, he could

17

hook me up. He lived with two roommates and barely answered his texts. We shared a love for *Star Wars* and good hamburgers. Luke meant well when we dated, but I wasn't sure if I could handle his carefree way of life. We remained friends with the occasional date. Nice guy, but not for the long haul.

"Um... I..." I managed to say. "Thank... you..."

What was going on? Why were two of my former boyfriends here?

"Can I come in?" Luke peeked over my shoulder.

"Um, sure." I fully opened the door and we ventured into my living room.

"Hey, Reese, are you--" Mateo's voice called from the kitchen doorway.

Oh no! Mateo and Luke were coming face to face. Would they fight over me? Would they both storm out? Or worse, would they compare notes about me? I refused to apologize for the number of notches in my bedpost, but I didn't want to make it common knowledge.

"Oh, you have company," Luke said as Mateo entered the room.

"Yeah, I..." I raked a hand through my long blonde hair. My headache pulsed under my fingers.

"Hi, I'm Mateo." Mateo, who was now thankfully for Luke's sake wearing a t-shirt, offered a hand to Luke.

"Luke." He shook Mateo's hand.

"How do you know Reese?" Mateo asked him.

Please, please, please don't tell him we ended up in bed on our first date. Even though Mateo and I weren't exclusive, he didn't need to know about my other bedroom adventures.

"My grandma is friends with her neighbah and they introduced us," Luke replied. Luke was born and raised in Providence, dropping his r's like any self-respecting New Englander. He set the paper bag and cup on my coffee table.

The men made themselves comfortable on my couch. I took a seat in a nearby chair, watching them warily.

Whew. Luke's response was the truth, but that's all Mateo needed to know. I still didn't understand why they were both here. I had no memory of texting either of them.

"Cool," Mateo said. He leaned back into my couch, placing an ankle on his opposite knee.

"Reese, you eating your muffin?" Luke pointed to the brown bag in front of me.

19

"Mateo made me--" I caught myself. "I mean sure." I grabbed the bag and opened it, taking a bite out of a warm blueberry muffin. A bite-sized orgasm. Luke remembered my favorite.

"Did you catch the Sox game the other night?" Mateo asked Luke.

I stopped chewing, in awe that Mateo treated Luke like one of his friends and that Luke felt at ease enough to drop himself on my couch. They had just met! I was curious about the texts they mentioned but didn't want to be a bad host or, worse yet, leave them alone to talk about me.

"Yeah," Luke replied. "Pedroia's on his way out." That was the consensus for most die-hard Red Sox fans. Dustin Pedroia had been with the team since 2006 and was a fan favorite, but his days were clearly numbered with a batting average of .100. Mateo had brought me to a few games and I had paid attention.

Even though we lived a good hour from Fenway, we cheered on the Sox. Those heathens 15 minutes away in Johnston rooted for the Yankees, citing an intra-city battle. Most of Providence rooted for the Patriots, though. When Gronk retired in 2018, the city mourned. Businesses closed for the day and residents clad in

20

black dragged their feet around town. When Tom Brady left for the Sunshine State, longtime football fans cursed his name. The GOAT quarterback had the initials "T.B." and moved to Tampa Bay with the same letters. Coincidence?

As I munched on my muffin and sipped some coffee, the guys talked about baseball stats and upcoming games. The mini meal helped ease my throbbing headache. I never did eat the eggs and bacon that Mateo made me. I felt like an outsider in the guys' conversation.

My phone rang from the kitchen and caught my attention.

"I'll be right back," I told the guys, thankful for the reprieve from a surreal and awkward moment.

I stepped into the kitchen and snatched my phone from the counter.

I grumbled at the random number from Sacramento and let the caller go to voicemail. Stupid spam callers asking me if I wanted to renew my car warranty. No thanks.

While the guys talked in the other room, I made a quick call to Ebony. Maybe she could help me figure out what was going on.

"Hey girl," I said when she picked up on the second ring.

"Why are you calling me already?" Ebony moaned. "It's not even 9:00. You complain when I text you this early. Good thing I'm done with my breakfast meeting."

Ebony and I met when I interviewed for a job with her when I moved back to Providence a few years ago. She didn't give me the job, but we bonded over the same restaurants we frequented and our love for shoes. She called me a few days later and wanted to hang out with me. We had been great friends ever since. She was one of the smartest people I knew.

"I had to call you," I whispered. I poked my head around the corner and saw Mateo and Luke still deep in conversation about sports. I stepped into the blind corner of the kitchen. "You'll never guess who's in my house."

"Who?"

"Mateo and Luke." The headache pulsed in my temples and I squeezed my eyes shut for a moment to relieve the pain.

"Mateo and Luke, the guys you used to date?" Ebony gasped. "Why did you invite them at the same time?"

Leave it to Ebony to ask the obvious.

"I didn't," I squealed, trying hard to keep my voice low. "They both showed up here."

"You didn't invite them over for a threesome?"

I imagined Ebony cocking her head at me.

"No, I swear. I think I'd remember if I did something like that." Admittedly, the thought had crossed my mind in the past year to experiment, but last night was not one of those times.

"Well, only when you're sober…"

"I *was* sober! I drove you home last night, remember?"

"I remember," Ebony jested. "How are they together? Are they doing any alpha-dog crap? Trying to one-up each other?"

"No, no, it's not like that." I poked my head around the corner again and peeked at the guys for a moment. "It's weird. They're talking sports in my living room and acting like they've been best friends for years."

"Where are you?"

"In the kitchen. They don't know I called you. I don't know why they're here. And I'm so afraid they'll share stories about me. I'd die." I wanted to go back to bed and start the day over.

"Girl, what did you do? Upset the Tinder gods?"

"I don't know," I sighed and struggled to open the old window to let in some fresh air. "Maybe I swiped left too many times and didn't match anyone. Then the wizard behind the curtain decided this was payback for me being too picky?"

My doorbell rang, echoing through the house.

"Somebody's at my door," I said. "I'll call you back." I hung up with Ebony, rushed past Mateo and Luke who gave me a quick nod while they were still deep in conversation, and walked to my front door. Another customer at the drive-thru?

Could this morning get any worse?

CHAPTER 3

Darnell.

I'll take Former Lovers for $600, Alex.

Darnell and I met before I dated Mateo. He was a chef at Camille's on Federal Hill and I felt terrible for sending back an undercooked steak. When Darnell came out of the kitchen to console me, the dissatisfied patron, he seemed pleasantly surprised when he approached my table. His jaw dropped and he complimented my dress. Darnell grabbed a chair from a nearby empty table and pulled it up next to me as if he'd done it a thousand times. We chatted for the next fifteen minutes until the kitchen staff called him back to work. He was different from most of the other guys I dated. He was kind and selfless. He had zero drama and didn't mind hanging out with my girlfriends and me. He gave me space but still wanted to spend time with me. Darnell didn't just say *Hey* when he texted me; he wrote sentences. A month after our first date, Darnell confessed that I was the sexiest steak scrutinizer he had ever met.

One night, Darnell and I talked about anything and everything until the early hours of the morning. He was incredibly easy to talk to and I felt at ease with him. He never judged me but called me out on my nonsense when I deserved it. Most guys didn't have the cajones to do that. I admired him for that.

Once, when I had a meltdown over a simple piece of cake, he patiently waited for me to finish crying and gave me a big hug. He'd often bring me iced coffee in the mornings on his way to work and cook for us at night. I didn't even mind that he playfully made fun of me because I didn't cook. He was on a mission to teach me even though I was an utter failure. He had talked about owning a restaurant and I encouraged him to do it. We shared secrets of our biggest fears and the first people who broke our hearts. I found comfort with him that I had never felt before or since. He was one of my favorite people.

He had told me he wanted to take care of me and share things with me. His quiet intelligence and confidence charmed me. One time, Darnell surprised me with a beautiful pair of raw emerald drop earrings. He explained that the color matched my green eyes. He purposely chose the drop kind because he had studied my Facebook posts and learned what I liked to wear. Wow, he was a keeper. Not only did he have good taste, but he took the time and effort to figure out what I would like.

After six months of dating, my stupidity got the best of me. I ended things with Darnell because I didn't think I was ready for an exclusive relationship. I freaked out because I was too afraid that he would dump me. I was terrified he wouldn't like the real me and I didn't want to get hurt. Dating experts would call me a classic runner. Ironic since I ran track in high school. I couldn't handle rejection. Scars of a bad relationship a few years earlier still affected me. Anger about that relationship resurfaced every once in a while. I needed complete closure from that before I could move on.

Darnell and I bumped into each other a few times since I ended things and we sent the occasional text over the past year, but nothing came to fruition. Looking back, Darnell was the one who got away. Ending things with him was the biggest mistake of my life. I appreciated more about Darnell because I experienced less without him.

"Hey, Reese." He smiled at me, his perfect white teeth contrasting against his dark skin. The beginnings of a beard speckled his chin. His dark hair was cut into a line-up. He could pass for John Legend who had gone a month without a trim. One night when we were out at a club, several women came up to him asking for the famous musician's autograph. Although flattered, Darnell politely turned them down.

In one swift motion, Darnell pulled me into a quick hug and kissed me on the cheek. I had forgotten how nice his hugs were. Did he miss me?

"What are you doing here?" I cringed, knowing that Luke and Mateo were already in my house.

"You asked me to come see you. I was already on this side of town, so I figured I'd stop by. Is everything okay?"

Had I somehow invited him over as well? I needed to figure everything out, but I didn't want to be rude and leave Darnell alone on my porch. I hadn't seen him in a couple of months and wanted to be appreciative of his impromptu visit. Besides, I couldn't get enough of his warm eyes.

"Yes, I'm fine. Thank you. Please, come in." As I opened the door to him, my headache hammered my brain. Since Mateo and Luke were already getting along, maybe Darnell would take their cue and be amicable too? I silently prayed to the Tinder gods to help me. Maybe Ebony was on to something? What had I done?

When Darnell spied Mateo and Luke on my couch, he stopped in place.

"I'm sorry, I didn't know you had company." He narrowed his eyes on me.

"Hi. Have a seat." Luke offered his hand to Darnell. "I'm Luke and this is Mateo."

Darnell glanced back at me, then shook Luke's hand. He greeted Mateo as well. Darnell sat in the chair that I had vacated. I stood in the corner, chewing on my fingernail.

What was going on? Why were three guys I had dated all in my living room, claiming that I invited them over? I went to bed last night at 11:30. Alone. I was sure of it. I should have checked my texts while I was on the phone with Ebony. Mental head slap.

As Luke and Mateo continued their conversation about the Red Sox batting averages, Darnell answered when spoken to, but didn't proactively contribute to the sports talk. He shifted in his seat and was unnaturally quiet. His discomfort silently screamed at me.

Darnell locked my gaze from across the small room and I grasped what he was thinking. Guilt coiled through my headache.

"Reese, I gotta go," he said to me. He stood from the chair and said his goodbyes to Mateo and Luke.

I escorted him to the front door and we stepped onto the front porch. Darnell shuffled his feet on the wooden floor.

The cool summer morning blew a nippy breeze at us --typical for this time of year. August weather in Rhode Island took on bipolar tendencies. It could be 80 degrees one day and 60 the next. Some dedicated surfers in Newport didn't care and jumped into the cold ocean anyway.

"I'm sorry." I raised a hand to my forehead.

"It's okay, I didn't tell you I was coming when you asked me to stop by."

"What?" I blinked. "When did I do that?"

"Last night. You texted me at midnight asking me to come over. I got it this morning. Don't you remember?"

I stumbled back against the porch rail. My eyes blinked rapidly as I tried in vain to process what he said. Luke and Darnell said something similar. Two times was a coincidence but three times was a pattern. Darnell reached for me and caught my fall.

"You okay?" he asked.

Wow, he was a good guy. One of the few. Even though catching my fall was a minor event, it added up to a wonderful man. One night, when I hadn't seen my friends in a few weeks, Darnell insisted that we take a girls' trip. When he and I had sex, he always made a point to make me feel special by wrapping me in his warm body and kissing my neck. Sex was good, but not knock-around like with Mateo.

"I don't know," I replied, peeling myself from his arms. My words were shaky and I swayed slightly. "All I know is that my head is throbbing and I don't remember

31

asking you to come over. I'm sorry if I made you uncomfortable with the other guys."

"It's fine." Darnell flicked a hand toward me. "I wasn't sure what you wanted when you asked me to stop by. Since your text was so late, I wanted to make sure you were okay. But I gotta go."

I needed to check my phone.

"Thanks for coming by. It was good to see you," I said.

"You too," Darnell said. "We should get coffee or something."

"I'd like that." I smiled.

Darnell hugged and kissed me on the cheek again before he walked off my porch. Then he left. At least he still wanted to hug me. I guess his annoyance at being around Luke and Mateo had dissipated. So had my guilt.

As I gazed down the street watching Darnell drive off, Luke and Mateo pushed through my front door. Mateo now wore shoes.

"Reese, we're heading out," Luke spoke for both of them. "I gotta get to the marina and Mateo's hitting the gym." They formed a small triangle around me.

"Okay, thanks for bringing me breakfast, and making me breakfast," I said. "Sorry I never ate the eggs, Mateo."

"No prob," he said. "Next time." He winked at me.

Both guys gave me a quick hug and stepped off my porch to their cars parked on the street.

As soon as they were out of sight, I rushed inside to check my phone for those crazy texts.

CHAPTER 4

In the kitchen, I snatched up my phone. I paced the room and pulled up the texts. My heart raced. I couldn't imagine what I wrote to the guys.

A text to Mateo at 11:53 p.m. You up?

That was our code phrase for "Do you want to come over for sex?" I slapped a hand to my forehead. Ow. My aching head.

Mateo responded at 11:57. Be there in 20.

A text to Luke at 11:59 p.m. I'm starving and I added a hungry face emoji. I cringed and rubbed an imaginary itch on my arm.

Luke didn't respond. Typical of him. But to his credit, he had brought me my favorite muffin and an iced coffee.

A text to Darnell at 12:02 a.m. How are you? Stop by sometime. Let's hang. At least he didn't reply with "Who's this?" I would have died.

But there they were. The three texts corroborated my actions and prompted all three men to come to my house at the same time. I wanted to crawl back in bed and start the day over. But why did I do it? I had no recollection of texting one of them, let alone three.

Maybe Mateo was right. Maybe someone slipped a roofie in my seltzer. Ebony, Jenna, Val, and I camped at the same table all night. It's not like we were mingling around a dance club where a creep could easily drop a pill in my drink. I couldn't imagine it was the bartender. With her super-tight tank top, she probably got better tips from the men in the bar. That wouldn't be reason enough to drug me, would it? The girls and I didn't order any food so that would eliminate any would-be assailant from the kitchen staff.

I poured myself a glass of water and gulped it down. Things did not make sense even though the water helped relieve the twisted knots in my head. I hunkered down at one of the kitchen countertops. What happened last night? Why didn't I remember anything?

I called Ebony back.

"Who was at your door?" she asked without giving me a chance to say hello.

"Darnell."

"What?? Darnell who you stupidly let go?"

"Don't remind me," I moaned.

"If I wouldn't violate the sisters before misters code, I'd go after him myself. He's a keeper. That brother is *fine*."

"Again, don't remind me." I refilled my glass and took a sip.

"What was he doing at your place?"

"He said he was on this side of town and stopped by because I asked him to."

"Just like Mateo and Luke?"

"Yes. Mateo came for sex and Luke came to feed me." I chewed my lower lip. "I gotta ask. Could my drink have been roofied last night?"

"I don't think so. Why?"

"Because I sent all three guys texts last night around midnight and I don't remember any of it." I

36

rubbed my temples, in a vain attempt to press out the stress of why I felt drugged and not because of my headache--which was slowly getting better.

Ebony was silent for a moment. "No, I don't remember anything weird happening. Did you ask Val and Jenna?"

"No, I haven't talked to them yet."

"Let me know what you find out and call me later."

"Okay. Later."

I hung up with Ebony and saw that Mateo had washed the pans he had used for the eggs and bacon as they were now standing upright in my drying rack. He had also put the dishes and forks in the dishwasher. He was a good guy, but I never felt that special connection with him. Being a nice person didn't always warrant being a boyfriend. He would make someone a great boyfriend, but it wasn't me. I liked him, but I didn't love him. I was pretty sure he felt the same way about me. In the meantime, he could give me an ego boost any time he wanted. He more than made up for me being friend-zoned in high school by the boys because I was a lean runner and didn't have Val's curves. One time, Mateo and I didn't even make it into the bedroom. He hoisted me onto the kitchen counter and we had at it. If Mrs. Patterson was watching from across the yard, she got quite the show.

At 80, Mrs. Patterson meant well despite her wanting to know way too much about my personal life. Even though I had moved away and came back to town, she still considered me a local and didn't snub me like the out-of-state transplants. Mrs. Patterson's husband had died a few years back so she was all alone in the white Cape Cod where a hedge separated our houses. Mr. Patterson was a fisherman and loved old ships. The massive anchor in the middle of their front yard displayed his obsession.

I looked out the window and Mrs. Patterson waved to me from her patch of zinnias.

"Good morning, Reese," she called. A proud Providence-for-lifer, she had that high-pitched nasal voice that local women often possessed. Her pink and white striped nightgown grazed the tops of her flowers. I cringed, imagining what was underneath.

"Hi, Mrs. Patterson," I projected my voice through the open window. Like other old people, I was never sure if she could hear me.

"I see you had a busy morning already with your boyfriends." She pointed toward my now empty porch.

"It's not what you think." I gnawed my lower lip. Who else on the block witnessed the pack of men on my porch earlier? If I wasn't careful, I'd be known as the town trollop.

"It nevah is, deeyah." She grinned at me with a mouthful of perfect white dentures. "How is that cute Porta-geese?" She was referring to Mateo since he hailed from the Portuguese locals who originally settled in Fox Point just across the Seekonk River.

"He's good. He left for the gym."

"He can come to my gym any time," she cackled.

Would Mateo be mortified or flattered that an 80-year-old woman lusted after him? Knowing Mateo, probably flattered.

"Have a good day, Mrs. Patterson," I called. "I'll talk to you later."

"You too, deeyah." She waved a gloved hand and turned back to her flower garden. Mrs. Patterson meant well, but like a lot of 80-year-old women, she was nosy, too.

I walked away from the window and headed upstairs. Mrs. Patterson was right. I did have a busy

39

morning and I needed to reward myself with a hot shower.

After I undressed and tossed my sweatshirt, tank top, and shorts into my dirty laundry basket, I grabbed a fresh towel from the linen closet and headed for the bathroom.

I hung the towel on the hook near the shower and caught a glance at my bathroom wastebasket. There it was. The miscreant that caused me to send those unsolicited texts and why my entire mind was blank.

CHAPTER 5

An empty bottle of Ambien.

"Oh my god!" I clapped a hand to my mouth.

A month ago, insomnia plagued me and my doctor prescribed Ambien. I completely forgot about it. I must have taken one (or several) last night. That explained my horrendous headache, the bizarre texts, and why I mistakenly left my phone in the kitchen.

The internet ran rampant with memes of Riding the Ambien Walrus. A rudimentary-drawn walrus tempted a poor sap into texting his ex-girlfriends, eating four pounds of cookies, buying a trumpet, and building a time machine out of old computer parts. The walrus promised an adventure nobody would remember. At least I had only texted three men. It could have been worse. A lot worse.

I exhaled and turned on the shower. The irritable pipes sputtered a few times and then spewed out a solid stream of water. Ah, the fun of owning an old house.

The drumming of the hot water on my face eased my aching head. After my shower, my headache was gone. I dressed in a long-sleeved white t-shirt and cut-off shorts. I slipped my feet into some Birkenstocks and headed downstairs.

In the kitchen, I picked up my phone and saw a new text from Mateo. Good to see you even though you fell asleep. Wanna make it up to me?

I barked a laugh. His boldness never ceased to amaze me.

Sure, I texted. I couldn't say no to him. He could rock my world any time. Besides, he had already made me eggs. I was a sucker for a man who cooked for me.

I'm working tomorrow. Lunch Monday? he wrote.

Monday is good, I replied. And this time I remembered typing it.

I dialed Val. She and I went to elementary, middle, and high school together. When I attended Villanova, she stayed local at the University of Rhode Island. We had kept in touch while in college and I'd see her occasionally after graduation. When I moved back to town three years ago, we picked up right where we left off, talking every day and getting together once a week.

"Hi, Val."

"Hey, girl."

"You'll never believe the morning I had. Mateo, Luke, AND Darnell were here."

"What? All at the same time? When did this happen? You were with us until 11," she talked faster than my brain could process.

"Yes. I was mortified."

"Why did you invite them all together?"

"I didn't. Well, I did. I didn't mean to though. I must've popped a couple Ambien, because I don't remember texting them."

"Girl, you're a mess," Val tsked me.

"I know." I shook my head in shame.

"How did the guys take it? Did they compare stories about you?"

43

"No, not at all. It was weird. Luke and Mateo were talking about the Sox. Darnell skipped out early though."

"Because he didn't want to be part of the foursome."

I cringed. "Yeah, probably."

"We still on for your birthday on Saturday?"

"Absolutely. I can't believe I'll be 30," I moaned.

"Welcome to the club," Val chimed. She loved to brag that she was six months older than me.

"I'll talk to you later. Tell Aidan I said hello." Val married her college sweetheart. They both enjoyed hiking along the coast in matching Vineyard Vines sweatshirts with their yellow lab Charlotte; they were perfect for each other.

When I hung up with Val, a text from Luke popped up on my screen. Dinner Monday?

I had lunch plans with Mateo, but dinner would work.

Sounds fun, I replied.

Harry's Bar at 5? Luke wrote.

`Works for me. See u then.` Getting two texts in a row from Luke was like seeing an opossum in daylight. I didn't want to scare him off.

I sent a quick text to Jenna saying I had lots to tell her. I'd see her at work on Monday morning and would fill her in with the details. Lots of things were happening on Monday.

CHAPTER 6

On Monday morning, I dressed for work in a navy-blue flared dress that looked like it lost a fight in a field of wildflowers. One of my favorites, the dress dipped into a V on my chest and hugged my curves. It always made me feel sexy. Hopefully, Mateo and Luke would take the hint. I touched up my eyelashes with some mascara and added some waves to my otherwise straight blonde hair with a flat iron. Some of my co-workers complained about the in-office rule of being presentable, but I didn't mind dressing up. I slipped my feet into some strappy sandals, grabbed my bag, and headed out the door.

After graduating from Villanova, I stuck around Philadelphia for a while, hoping that my writing career would take off. After five years of dead-end day jobs and a horrible breakup, I tucked my tail between my legs and came home to Providence. Every once in a while, thoughts of that disastrous relationship crept into my head. When that happened, my chest tightened and I wanted to hurl a fire hydrant at someone. After a few creative expletives and a pulsing vein in my forehead, Ebony usually talked me off a ledge. In a cruel twist of fate, maybe that relationship prevented me from having a stable one now? Did I have a fear of commitment because I didn't want to go through something like that again?

I may have had an awkward living room full of ex-boyfriends two days earlier, but it was nothing compared to the ex I left in Philly.

I moved back three years ago and interviewed for a job with Ebony's agency. When that path didn't work out, I landed a legal assistant position at a lobbying firm. The salary would never help me buy a mini mansion in Federal Hill, but I loved my team. Especially Jenna.

Fifteen minutes later, I was motoring along in the middle of downtown Providence in my late grandma's old car. It was a royal blue 1970 Chevy Impala. The original bench vinyl seats had been mended a few times, but I refused to replace them because the car still smelled like her. Old and musty. I loved it. In the summer, I hand-cranked the windows open because it lacked air conditioning. Driving in the snow was the worst because it had rear-wheel drive. Parallel parking was hardly an option because of its massive length. My car was longer than some small trucks. Despite my mechanic's urging me to upgrade to an automatic or something that didn't have a gear shift on the floor, I would drive it until it fell apart. It was my last connection to my grandma.

On Westminster Street, the "Superman Building" towered above me. The tallest skyscraper earned its nickname because it resembled the *Daily Planet* from the Superman comics. City officials had argued back and forth for years about renovating it. Demolishing the art-deco building was not an option since it resided within feet of neighboring structures. While waiting on a decision, the building had been vacant since 2013.

I parked my car two blocks away in the Biltmore Garage. Then, I headed towards my building on Dorrance Street. Along the way, I grabbed an iced coffee from the nearby Dunkin' and threaded my way in and out of other folks heading to work. Honking trucks blocked traffic while making early morning deliveries. Smoky car exhaust filled the late summer air. Uniformed doormen assisted patrons in and out of high-end condos. A bicycle delivery boy zipped past me, nearly knocking me down.

"Crazy biker!" I shouted and shook a fist at him.

Minutes later, I reached my building, climbed the stairs to the third floor, and pushed through the office doors.

Jenna perched behind the oak reception desk, a headset on her blonde locks. A small strand of dyed hair peeked out from under her ear. This month it was pink. Last month it was purple. The month before that it was blue. Across from her desk was a coffee table full of a kaleidoscope of glossy government magazines. Framed artwork accented the white walls. A hallway behind Jenna led to our maze of cubicles and offices. Someone would need a GPS to find me in the middle.

A transplant from South Carolina, Jenna left Charleston after college and followed an ex-boyfriend to Providence. He dumped her a few months later, but she didn't want to go back home and be marked a failure by her impossible-to-please parents. I consoled her the morning after the breakup and we had been great friends ever since. We compared dating stories, shopped together, got coffee after work, and were each other's +1 for parties. She always offered a positive spin to any story and I loved her for that.

"Mornin' sunshine," Jenna squealed, peeking over her monitor. "Sounds like you had a busy morning with three hot men in your house!"

I groaned. "Let's just say I was riding the Ambien Walrus."

"Oh no." Jenna cupped her mouth with a hand. "What did you do?"

I filled her in on the details of my Saturday morning with Mateo, Luke, and Darnell.

"Now what? Are you seein' any of the guys again?" Jenna asked, her soft Southern drawl coming through.

"Yes," I explained, "I'm meeting Mateo at lunch today and am having dinner with Luke tonight."

"How fun. Where ya meetin' Mateo?" She grabbed a pen from a nearby jar and twirled it through her pink and blonde hair.

"I don't know yet. Hopefully, he'll text me later this morning."

"And Luke?"

"Harry's on Main. How do I look?" I did a mini twirl in front of her, showing off my dress.

"You're a bit overdressed for a burger joint, but if the guys aren't starin' at you, then they're gay," Jenna laughed. "Believe me, I should know."

"Aw, don't be so hard on yourself," I consoled her. "It was one time."

"I'd like to think I'd know if a man is gay or not," Jenna moaned. "I think my gaydar is off." Jenna had dated a guy for six months and never had a clue that he was gay until he told her he was into guys.

"Maybe he hid it well or he was lying to himself," I offered. "How were you supposed to know?"

"I had no idea," Jenna said. "I guess him taking way too long at the weekly pant fittings at the men's suit store should have clued me in. You'd think I'd pick up on something!"

I stifled a laugh.

"You'll find someone again soon, I'm sure of it." I glanced at the clock on the wall above her head. "I gotta go. I have to get some spreadsheets done by eleven."

A few of our colleagues wandered in and said good morning to us.

"Let me know how your lunch goes with Mateo if I don't see you before then," Jenna called out as I headed down the hall to my desk.

My desk was in the middle of the cube farm. Tan, soft-sided dividing walls separated my co-workers from me; our metal nameplates perched on top. My wire inbox was filled with documents to review. Pictures of my friends and parents splattered my corkboard, an unwrapped granola bar stuck to my desk, and a sad-looking plant silently screamed for sunlight from the corner shelf.

I got to work replying to emails, answering calls, and typing up documents.

At 10:30, Mateo texted me, Paco's Tacos food truck at 12:30?

I'll be there, I typed back.

Paco's Tacos was usually parked on the next block, so it was a quick walk for me. I spent the next two hours holed up at my desk reviewing documentation

from the firm's lobbyists and attorneys, counting the minutes until I could see Mateo. Things were easy with Mateo because no feelings were involved. I needed to see him, especially on a Monday.

Some of my co-workers walked by to grab printouts from the printer, but I kept my mind focused on my work so that I could get everything done and enjoy lunch with Mateo. I gradually depleted the pile of papers on my desk.

At 12:25, I bolted from my desk, taking the stairs as fast as I could in my heels. I set off down the sidewalk to meet Mateo. The late August sun warmed my face. Nothing that a dose of Vitamin D couldn't fix.

Five minutes later, I found him waiting for me at the end of a short line for Paco's Tacos. He wore a white moisture-wicking workout t-shirt, his muscles begging to get out. Wow, he was hot. I blew out a low whistle in his direction.

"You look great." Mateo's eyes lit up and he peck-kissed me on the mouth.

"Thank you." I did a mini curtsey for him. "You too."

"If you don't mind, can we take our food to-go? I'd like to show you something." A few beads of sweat glistened along the edge of his dark hair.

"Yeah, sure," I said.

We placed our orders for a couple of tacos, Mateo paid, and we munched on them as we walked down the sidewalk. On the next block, we stopped in front of an empty four-story office building. "For Lease" signs splattered the ground floor windows.

"This is it," Mateo said as he popped the last bite of taco into his mouth.

"There's nothing here," I stated the obvious.

"I signed the lease for the first-floor last month," Mateo said, as the corners of his mouth curved up. "I'm opening my own gym here."

"Wow! That's great!" I mumbled as I chewed the remains of my taco and gave him a quick hug. "I'm so happy for you. You are such a great trainer!"

"Wanna see it?"

"Yes." I grinned at him, hoping that no remnants of lettuce remained in my teeth.

Mateo pulled a jingling keychain out of his pocket and led me to the front door. He opened it up, waited until I entered the building, and then locked the door behind us.

As we walked into the main area, the aroma of fresh-cut lumber and new paint permeated my nose. Panels of drywall rested against framed walls. I expected to hear hammers pounding and drills whirring but didn't.

"Where's the construction crew?" I asked.

"Out to lunch," Mateo replied. "Let me show you around."

"Okay."

"I'm putting the weight machines here." He pointed to the massive open space in the front and then led me toward the back of the room.

"Sounds great." I nodded as I took it all in.

"And I'll put the treadmills and bikes here." Mateo held his arms wide in the back corner.

"I'm sure it'll be the bomb."

"Do you want to see where I'll do private training sessions?"

"Sure." I bobbed my head up and down.

Mateo quickly grabbed my hand and guided me toward a room that was sectioned off by two-by-fours. Heavy plastic draped from the ceiling. In one swift

55

motion, Mateo pushed me against a new piece of drywall.

"This is where I'll be able to have one-on-one sessions," Mateo whispered in my ear. He slid a hand up and down my sides, curling his finger under the edge of my dress.

"If I get one, we'll have to be sure we lock the door," I murmured.

"You are so hot, Reese. Total smoke show," Mateo said, his hand edging up my thigh. "When I first saw you in that dress, I knew I had to have you. You are mouthwatering."

My face burned crimson.

"We have about twenty minutes before I need to go back to work," I purred.

"I only need fifteen." He leaned further into my small frame. "I love that you are fun-size."

Mateo kissed my lips and pressed his hard body against mine. I moaned in response and widened my legs. He reached higher up underneath my dress, slid my panties off, and let them fall to the floor. He then pushed the front of his track pants down, hoisted me up, and found his way inside me...

56

CHAPTER 7

Twenty minutes later, after the quickie with Mateo, I scurried up the stairs to my office. I sniffed myself, unsure if his scent would give away the fact that we had sex. God, he was hot. I lost all control when I was with him. He could turn a nun. Even though a real relationship would go nowhere with him and we remained friends, I took full advantage of the benefits. Hot, but not for me.

"How was lunch with Mateo?" Jenna caught my attention as I pushed through the main doors.

"Amazing." I grinned so wide my face hurt.

"Girl, if I didn't know any better, I'd think you had sex with him."

57

I wiggled my eyebrows at Jenna.

"You did!" she gasped and slapped the desk separating us. "Where did you go in the past hour? It's not like you can easily go back to your house and get it on. Or did you get a hotel room?" Jenna narrowed her eyes at me.

"He brought me to a building a couple of blocks away that he's renovating for a new gym," I explained. I patted my cheeks, checking to see if they were still warm. "And then we..." I hesitated saying too much in case any of our co-workers were within earshot. Some of the stodgy attorneys were old-school fifth generation and probably didn't want to hear about my sexcapades.

Jenna laughed and shook her head at me. "You crack me up."

I couldn't help but laugh myself.

"Are you still seein' Luke after work?" Jenna asked.

"Yeah, at 5:00. Hopefully, he shows up. I haven't heard from him all day. But that's typical of him." I rolled my eyes. "I'll leave from here since it'll be dumb for me to go all the way home to the east side and come back again. Normally I'd walk the half-mile, but not in these shoes." I pointed to the strappy sandals on my feet that

58

were already aching from the two-block walk to Mateo's new gym.

"There's street parking in front of Harry's, but if you can't find a spot, there's a lot a block away," Jenna offered.

"No way I'm squeezing into a tight spot with my car." I glanced at the clock on the wall. "I gotta go. Catch you later."

I spent the next few hours scheduling meetings, reviewing legal documents, investigating sources, and talking to legislators. I loved my job and the afternoon flew by.

Just after 4:00, I finally took a break and walked over to Jenna's desk. She held a finger up in a wait signal to me as she typed a few more sentences. She mouthed the words as she typed.

"Okay, I'm done for a minute. What's up?"

"Just wanted to say good night," I said.

"I'm leavin' here in about 20 minutes," Jenna replied. "You'll have to tell me all about your date with Luke tomorrow. Or text me if you get a chance."

"Don't worry, I will," I said with a smile. "I'm sure it won't be as hot as lunch with Mateo, but we'll still have fun. Luke's a good guy."

I walked away from Jenna and cringed about what I just said. Burgers at Harry's with Luke will be pretty tame compared to a nooner with Mateo. However, was Mateo's sex scent still on me? I would hate for Luke to pick up on it, even in a crowded, beer-infested pub.

How would I get rid of Mateo's scent? I didn't have time to go home and shower.

As I walked past the community kitchen, an idea came to me. Maybe I could find something in there to mask the trace of Mateo. I stepped into the small space and opened a drawer. Several dozen loose salt and pepper packets. That wouldn't do unless I wanted to sneeze all night. I pulled the next drawer open. Take out menus from downtown restaurants and caterers. The third drawer yielded unmatched serving utensils and kitchen tools. What was I going to do? As I opened an overhead cabinet, I closed my eyes, willing it to have a resolution within it. What was that old game show that had prizes behind the curtain? The Price is Right? Let's Make a Deal? Mrs. Patterson probably knew the answer.

I opened my eyes to a small set of vinegar and oil bottles. Perfect! Snatching the bottles from the shelf, I flipped open the dispenser caps and let a few drops of vinegar and oil fall onto my wrist. I rubbed my wrists together and pressed both of them against my neck. I now smelled like Caesar salad, but it was better than having Mateo's aroma on me. Feeling a sense of relief, I headed back to my desk to shut down my computer for the night.

* * * *

A half-hour later, I didn't even bother looking for street parking and found a stall in the nearby lot. No other cars were parked nearby and I easily slid in. I got out and walked along North Main Street to Harry's. The burger and beer joint found refuge in a three-story red brick building nestled between a paintball shop and dessert cafe. A few people enjoyed the warm August air at the powder blue sidewalk tables. The white metal sign above the door bragged that the bar was *Open Late*.

I pushed through the green wooden door and told the hostess that I'd be sitting at the bar. Luke wasn't there, but that didn't surprise me. The pub was half-full of patrons; some dressed in suits and dresses and others in more casual attire. A black and white cow pattern decorated the back half of the ceiling above the bar. Bottles of Tito's, Bacardi, Old Forester, and Johnnie Walker lined the shelves against the interior brick wall.

61

I slid onto an empty stool next to a grey-haired man dressed in overalls who was chatting up a bald man on the other side of him. After placing my draft order with the bartender, the grey-haired man tapped me on the shoulder.

"'Scuse me," he said, "my buddy and I are having an ahgument and maybe you can help settle it."

"Sure, I guess," I replied. He must've had a sixth sense that I was born and raised in Providence because it was a known fact that locals didn't strike up conversations with strangers.

"What's the best way to get to Atwood Grill?" he asked me.

"I--" Before I could utter another word, his smooth-headed friend interrupted me.

"You know," the bald man barked, "you go to that place that used tah be Palumbah's, then go three blahks and make a left at Mahty's brothah's place."

Who was Marty? And who was his brother?

"Nah, nah," the grey-haired man turned away from me and cut off his friend. "Go to where the old Benny's used tah be and head west on Route 6."

Their ridiculous debate made me dizzy, although I agreed with the grey-haired man.

The bartender slid a pint of Old Speckled Hen ale in front of me as a welcomed relief.

"Want something to eat?" he said to me. "You just missed happy hour for half-priced burgers."

"Yes, please," I replied as I took a sip. "Hopefully my friend is coming soon and I won't be eating alone."

"If not, I'm sure those guys would love your company." He chuckled and gestured to the old men next to me who were drowned in their conversation.

The bartender left me and I checked my phone. 5:10 and still no Luke. If he was any other guy, I would finish my beer and take off. But Luke was notorious for being late. I think he meant well but got so caught up in his work at the docks that he lost track of time. It wouldn't do me any good to text him because he wouldn't answer anyway. I probably would have had time to run home and shower, but it was too late now.

A few moments later, the bartender pushed a menu in front of me. Mmm. Burgers.

"Look at the giant freak with the long haiyah," the grey-haired man cackled, interrupting my watering mouth.

I turned and faced the entrance to see who they were talking about.

63

Luke.

He caught my gaze, smiled wide, and headed toward me.

"Hi, Reese," Luke said and settled into the empty stool next to me, his long legs folded under the lip of the bar. The two old-timers shook their heads at us and chuckled.

Luke gestured to my dress. "You look cute." I was batting a thousand.

"Thanks. I thought you were bailing on me again," I teased.

"Yeah, my mom says that all the time when she doesn't heyah from me for days."

I rolled my eyes. "Have you thought about calling her back when that happens?"

Luke shrugged and raked a hand through his shaggy hair. "Sometimes."

Getting Luke to respond to anyone promptly was like asking a fish to climb a tree. It wasn't happening so it wasn't worth the argument.

"You hungry?" I held the menu up.

"Stahved."

The bartender appeared in front of us and asked Luke, "What can I get you to drink?"

"Coronah," Luke replied. "Thanks, man."

"Be right back with that," the bartender said. "And I'll get your food order then."

Luke sniffed the air like a dog investigating a new scent. "Does it smell like a salad in heyah?"

I froze. He could smell the vinegar and oil on me! But at least he didn't pick up on Mateo's scent.

"I don't smell anything," I lied and cringed.

The bartender brought Luke's beer and set the bottle in front of him. A lime was stuffed into the top of the open bottle. Luke pushed the lime down into the beer.

"What can I get you to eat?" the bartender asked us.

"I'll take a bacon cheeseburger and a side of sweet potato fries," I said.

"And I'll take a pastrami buhgah and regulah fries," Luke told him.

"Sounds great," the bartender replied and wandered off to the ordering screen at the middle of the bar.

"Sorry they don't have any blueberry muffins for you," Luke added.

"Thanks for remembering they're my favorite," I said. He was a sweet guy.

"How do you know Mateo and what was the other guy's name? David?" Luke asked after our food came.

"Darnell." I wanted to crawl into my skin. My worst fear had come to fruition.

"Yeah, Dahnell," Luke said. "They seemed like good guys."

"They are," I agreed with a nod, silently relieved that Luke felt that way. I was not as embarrassed to tell him the truth. "I had dated both of them, but we're just friends now."

"Like you and me?"

"Yeah, like you and me."

"Cool."

A wave of relief came over me that Luke was satisfied with my answer. I was worried for nothing.

Luke and I spent the next two hours noshing on burgers and fries and downing some beers. We talked about the Red Sox, our mutual love of *Star Wars*, our families, work, and our first car accidents. He was a good guy, but his carefree lifestyle would never work for

66

me. I had a pretty easy-going lifestyle, but Luke going dark for days on end would drive me crazy.

CHAPTER 8

When I got home at 7:30, a medium-sized box from Amazon was sitting on my porch. I didn't remember ordering anything, but that didn't mean much. I was too cheap to pay for Prime and sometimes my orders would take weeks to be delivered and I'd forget about them. The August evening sun cast a long shadow on the box. I picked it up and shuffled it in my arms because it was heavier than I expected it to be. I unlocked my front door with my free hand and walked inside.

Once I set the box on my kitchen table, I grabbed a pair of scissors out of my junk drawer and sliced it open. I found two large bags of cereal marshmallows, like the ones in Lucky Charms.

What in the world?

On top of the plastic bags lay the ordering slip. I snatched it, unfolded it, and read a gift receipt: `Happy 30th Birthday Sweetie! Sorry we can't be there to celebrate with you. Love, Mom & Dad`

While I lived in Philadelphia, my parents had decided that Rhode Island was too cold for them. They packed up and moved to Boca Raton. When they learned I wanted to move back to Providence, they were thrilled that someone would be near my grandpa. At 82, he was still in good shape, but my mother worried that he needed someone close by just in case. A few years ago, he was in a minor fender-bender and my mother refused to let him renew his driver's license. If he didn't take the bus, I drove him to where he needed to go.

When I was younger, my dad often pranked me with practical jokes like tying my wrist to a light while I slept on the sofa or hiding my left shoe somewhere in the house, so eight pounds of cereal marshmallows wasn't out of his bag of tricks. My grandpa was a frequent co-conspirator.

I wasn't sure what I would do with the marshmallows, but there was no way I was eating them all. My coworkers were in for a treat.

I pulled my phone out of my purse and called Val.

"You'll never believe what my parents sent me," I said into the phone when she picked up.

"A shower curtain with a big cat on it?" Val laughed. "Your dad is a hoot."

I chuckled with her. "No."

Val continued, "I remember on Prom night when he opened the door to our dates wearing only a bow tie and black underwear."

"Oh my god, I forgot all about that," I laughed. "He said he was a Chippendales dancer but we didn't know what that was."

"More like a reject from Magic Mike," Val jested.

I winced at the memory of my dad's big belly hanging over his skimpy drawers.

"Good thing our dates thought it was funny," I recalled. "Otherwise, it would have been a long night."

"Anyway, what did your parents send you?" Val asked.

"Eight pounds of Lucky Charms marshmallows."

70

Val cackled into the phone. "That's freaking hilarious!"

"Yeah, I'm glad to see my dad hasn't lost his touch," I said.

"If they were still here, I'm sure he would do more," Val replied. "How often does his only child turn 30?"

"Well, once," I chuckled.

"I gotta go," Val interrupted me. "Aidan's asking me what I did with his keys."

"Maybe my dad took them?" I joked.

Val laughed and said goodbye.

I hung up with her and noticed a text notification from Darnell. I hadn't heard a word from him since Saturday morning when he encountered Mateo and Luke in my living room. That was two days ago.

He wrote: Good to see you. Have a good week.

His note was simple and platonic, but at least he made an effort to send the text in the first place. What was that saying again? If a guy didn't like you, he wouldn't even talk to you?

I replied: Good to see you too. Let me know if you want to get a beer or

71

something. In my mind, "or something" could mean more than just a beer, maybe even some fun making out or innovative ways of conditioning his beard. I wanted to leave it to his imagination and have him make the first move.

Sounds fun, he wrote.

Then nothing else for the rest of the night.

Ugh.

Even though he was the one who got away, I wasn't chasing him and begging for a date. Hell, I didn't even chase my whiskey.

CHAPTER 9

The next morning, I carried two big transparent bags of marshmallows to my office. Escaping weird looks from people on the sidewalk was hopeless.

"What is *that*?" Jenna shrieked when I walked in the door. She eyed my provisions.

"An early birthday gift from my parents." I plopped the giant bags on the reception desk in front of her.

"And you brought it all here?"

"Where else would I bring it?"

"I dunno." Jenna twirled the pink strand of hair in her fingers. "Maybe the food bank? So, all of the homeless people could have a fun breakfast?"

"Good idea! Can I keep them here until lunch when I can drop them off? I'm sure my parents won't mind if I share the wealth."

"Sure."

I pulled the bags from the desk and dropped them in the corner of the reception area.

"You still coming out for my birthday on Saturday?" I asked Jenna.

"I wouldn't miss it." She smiled at me.

"Val is driving so I can drink. Ebony is driving herself," I said. "She said she has to meet a client that afternoon. Someone who can't get together on a weekday."

"She's such a workaholic," Jenna laughed.

I nodded in agreement and headed to my desk to review discovery documentation.

* * * *

After work, Mrs. Patterson met me on the sidewalk at the edge of the hedge separating our houses. I had just plucked a few ripe tomatoes from my garden. She held out a small package from Amazon.

"This is for you, deeyah," she said. Pink, plastic hair rollers covered her silver locks.

"Oh, thank you." I took the box from her.

74

"The mail lady mistakenly put it in my mailbox."

"I'm sure it was an accident," I reassured her.

"I don't know…" Mrs. Patterson narrowed her eyes at me. "I don't trust the post office. I mailed something to my sistah in Arizona a week ago and she hasn't gotten it yet. They steal things."

I tried to stifle a laugh knowing that if any postal worker was caught stealing mail, they'd wind up in jail.

"I'm sure it will get to her."

Mrs. Patterson changed her suspicious facial expression to a sly grin. "How is that cute Porta-geese?"

"He's good. I saw Mateo yesterday." Hot memories of our quickie filled my thoughts.

"I hope to see him again soon too."

I shook my head at her and chuckled. If she was serious, Mateo could have a stalker with a walker on his hands.

"Well, I have to go. Have a good night, Mrs. Patterson."

"You too, deeyah."

I scurried into my house with the small package and an armful of tomatoes. In my kitchen, I tore it open and found four mini black and white striped socks, each sporting a smiley face. What the hell?

The packing slip said they were dog socks. Only I didn't have a dog.

I flipped open the gift receipt and read a note from my Aunt Jackie in Texas. Happy 30th Birthday Reese! I hope your dog will love these! Love, Aunt Jackie

My Aunt Jackie was known for her odd gifts. One year my mom got a Bob Ross chia pet from her sister for Christmas.

Rolling my eyes, I sent a quick text to my aunt thanking her for the unusual birthday present. It was the thought that counted, right? The dog socks will be added to my tub labeled "useless gifts".

The next few days brought more peculiar birthday gifts. A bag of unicorn farts from my cousin Freddy in Dallas. He was my dad's protege. Twelve pounds of cheese from my Uncle Charlie in Wisconsin. The cheese made sense, but I sure as hell didn't need 12 pounds. A single bag of Japanese tea from my cousin Julia in San Francisco. A life-size cutout of Danny DeVito from my college roommate Maureen. A bag of 100 tiny handcuffs from my other college roommate Niki.

My family and friends had a strange sense of humor, that was for sure.

CHAPTER 10

On Saturday at 7:15, Val picked me up in her 1972 Fiat 124 Spider. Her father restored the two-door powder blue roadster and presented it to her for her 30th birthday. Gee, my dad gave me eight pounds of cereal marshmallows. What was I doing wrong?

"You ready to go, Birthday Girl?" she called as I stepped off my porch. Her long brown hair fell into waves down her back. She wore a deep V-neck black t-shirt that showed off her voluptuous girls. She garnered a lot of attention from the boys in high school. "Jenna texted me she's on her way."

"Nice. And I'm ready!" I slid into the front seat next to her and put my seat belt on. "What's Aidan doing tonight?"

"Hanging out with the boys," Val said. "I told him I'd be out late and not to wait up."

Ten minutes later, we arrived at Wickenden Pub. The bar was on the ground floor of a three-story cedar clapboard building that could have been built by the original Colonists. We liked it because it was laid-back and intimate. The bartenders knew us and often gave us free samples of the global craft beers they had on tap.

When Val and I walked in, the round high tops were already full of members of the beer club. Jenna waved to us from the middle booth where her shoulder was against the primitive stone wall. Val settled in next to Jenna and I saved a seat for Ebony on the opposite side.

We ordered two pints of Narragansett for Jenna and me and seltzer for Val from the bartender. At the table closest to us, we overheard a man and woman talking. Both appeared to be in their mid-twenties.

"Betcha they're on a first date." Jenna nodded in the couple's direction.

"How can you tell?" Val asked. "How do you know it's a *first* date?"

"They're sitting a little farther apart like they aren't comfortable with each other yet," Jenna explained. Even though Jenna was four years younger than Val and me, she was just as perceptive as us. If not more.

The three of us glanced at the couple without moving our heads so that we didn't get caught rudely staring at strangers.

"And if you listen close enough," Jenna added, "you can hear that he's asking her first date questions like what movies she likes and where she's from."

I smirked at Jenna.

Moments later, Ebony stood at the entrance of the bar, scanning the room for us. She wore a white silk button-down blouse and a matching skirt that contrasted against her smooth brown skin. Her long dark hair was pulled together into dozens of tiny braids that fell down her back. She was tall and lean, the after-effects of running five miles a day. If I was into girls, I would call her a smoke show.

I waved her over to join us in the dimly lit side of the bar.

"Happy Birthday! Sorry I'm late," Ebony groaned as she hugged me and sat next to me. "I had to meet with some Masshole who thinks he'll be a starting third baseman for the Sox next year." Ebony was a sports agent and held her own in the male-dominated business. She grew up in Queens and her take-no-prisoners New York attitude stayed with her. No one dared to mess with her or they'd get an estrogen-fuel Molotov cocktail. We called Ebony The Queen of Queens. After spending a few years with the Mets organization, she wanted a change with the New England teams. She moved to Providence a couple of years before I came back.

When the bartender brought our drinks, Ebony ordered her usual, one snifter of Buffalo Trace Bourbon. Neat. It would last her the entire night.

"Aren't you driving?" I glowered at Jenna as she took a long sip of her beer.

"I Ubered here, *mom*."

"Sorry, I can't take you home," Val said to Jenna. "My car is only a two-seater. Unless you want to stuff yourself in the trunk."

"I can take you home," Ebony offered.

Jenna nodded toward the nearby couple again. "Oooh, that guy is not getting a second date."

The four of us glanced over to see the guy with his nose in his phone. His date silently glared at him; her annoyance filled the atmosphere of the bar.

"I feel your pain, sister," Ebony spoke to the woman, but only loud enough for us to hear. "One guy I dated couldn't stop staring at the waitress." She rolled her eyes. "Why are men so obtuse?"

"This guy I dated kept bragging about how good of a catch he was," I added. "He was a six at best."

"I remember him," Val said. "What was he? Like five-foot-five? Such a bold statement for a small guy."

"Sounds like a Napoleon Complex," Ebony said.

"Ironically, he lived in a town called Waterloo."

We howled in laughter.

Jenna pointed to Ebony. "Don't you get all the cute athletes?"

Ebony scoffed and shook her head. "Those guys are a bunch of arrogant dopes who show off their money and go through women like underwear. No thanks."

"At least you didn't date the guy who pulled his dick out on the first date!" I said. "Despite what they say, he was *not* hung like a horse." I waved my pinky at them and grimaced.

My friends groaned in the hilarity.

"Or that whack job I dated in Philly who made me wait six months for sex," I said.

"Or the 10-pump chump I had," Val added.

We gawked at her.

"*Before* I married Aidan," Val clarified. "That guy rolled off me and immediately fell asleep. I was like, that's it?" She held her hands up in a questioning gesture.

"At least you got married," I said. "I dated someone for two years in Philly and he kept saying how much he wanted to marry me but he never gave me a ring. I finally dumped him."

"You dodged a bullet with that one." Jenna motioned to me. "My first date in this town texted me from his car and said 'Here'. Back in Charleston, men were taught manners. They'd hold doors and say, 'Yes ma'am' and 'Yes sir.'"

"Sister, you're a long way from Charleston!" Ebony teased. "One guy I dated for a few months refused to meet my parents. I told him to put his big *girl* pants on and suck it up."

"Speaking of sucking," I said. "This one guy I knew barely went *downtown*. On the few times that he did, he did it all wrong."

"How'd he do it wrong?" Val asked me. "It's not that hard. You learn body parts in high school health class. I mean come on."

"He was here…" I pointed to my forehead. "And not here…" I pointed to my mouth. "After that, I was like stop, stop. It's not worth it."

My friends slapped the table in laughter. A few other customers gave us the death stare for being so loud and we quieted down.

"You had a guy who wouldn't go downtown." Ebony lowered her voice and gestured to me. "But I had a guy who didn't have a lot going on upstairs." She poked a finger to her head, sliding a few braid strands out of her way. "He didn't know what a tapas restaurant was or what hair mousse was. I had to explain to him how to pronounce the word alibi. He picked up my book *A is for Alibi* and said 'ah-lee-bee'. Uh, no. The lights were on, but nobody was home. He was a nice guy and he adored me, but I couldn't be his life tour guide."

"Speaking of nice guys, or lack thereof," Jenna said, pointing to herself. "One guy I dated back home boasted that he was a good boyfriend because he wasn't a drunk and didn't hit women."

"Um, men aren't *supposed* to do those things," Val commented.

"I hope you told him 'thanks for setting the bar so low,'" I sarcassed.

"No, but I dumped him soon after," Jenna replied.

"Good girl," Ebony said.

The bartender came to our table and interrupted our gabfest.

"You ladies doing okay?" he asked.

"Tomorrow is this girl's 30th birthday." Val gestured toward me. "Can you make her something special?"

"Happy Birthday." He nodded to me. "I don't have any champagne." The bartender wiped his hands on a rag that he pulled from his front jeans pocket. "But I can whip you up a Dirty Thirty."

"Oooh, what's that?" Jenna leaned forward on her elbows and asked the question we all wanted to know the answer to.

"Tito's and Sparkling Sauvignon Blanc," he replied.

"That sounds fun," I said. "Just two. One for me and one for my friend Jenna."

"Another seltzer for me." Val pointed to herself.

Ebony waved a hand over her barely touched bourbon. "I'm good."

The bartender walked off to get our drinks.

The girls and I spent the next few hours downing drinks and comparing our dating adventures. Between the four of us, we had plenty of experience and made no apologies for the long list of men in our beds.

After a half dozen cocktails, I slowly raised a hand to my forehead.

"You okay?" Ebony asked me.

"I- I- think so," I groaned. "Whaaaat time is it?"

Val glanced at her phone. "Midnight."

"We should go to a club dance," Jenna piped up and tried to get up from the inside corner of the booth.

Val laughed at her inebriated state and inability to form a correct sentence.

"That's it, you're cut off," Ebony declared to Jenna, "I'm taking you home." She slapped a hand on the table and I jumped from the unexpected noise. Ebony's long braids danced to the sound.

A few minutes later, my friends split the bill as a birthday gift to me and we headed to the door. However, Jenna and I did not follow the rule that the shortest distance between two points was a straight line.

CHAPTER 11

The next morning, I pulled myself out of bed, groaning from a hangover. At least this time I knew why my body ached. Six drinks would knock anyone out. As I slouched on the edge of the bed and ran fingers through my hair, my phone rang on the nightstand. I picked it up and recognized the caller.

"Good morning birthday girl!" my mom sang into the phone.

I winced. How could someone be so cheery this early in the morning?

"Hi, Mom."

"How are you spending your big day?"

"I have a couple errands to run. Then I'm visiting Grandpa later for an early dinner."

"Tell him we miss him and send our love. Hold on, sweetie, your dad wants to get on the line."

I glanced at the clock while I waited. 9:30. I was sure my dad had already been up since six and spent the early morning fishing at the pier.

"'Morning, baby girl," he said. "Happy birthday."

"Thanks, Dad."

"How's my favorite child?"

"Good, Dad." This was a running joke ever since I could remember. My dad purposely called me his favorite child when we were out in public simply to get a reaction from anyone nearby. The joke was that I was his *only* child.

"Did you get the gift we sent you?"

"Yes, I did. Very funny. Ha-ha. This could be your best one yet."

"It's what you asked for."

"Huh?"

"What?"

"Why would I want eight pounds of cereal marshmallows?" I shook my head and sat upright. My dad had my attention.

"I don't know. I was wondering the same thing."

"When did I ask for it?"

"On your Amazon gift wish list."

"What?" I shrieked. "What Amazon gift wish list? I never made one."

"Yes, you did. It said the list was created last Friday night."

"Oh my god." I clapped a hand to my mouth. Another surprise from the Ambien walrus. What else lay ahead for me?

"What's wrong?"

"I took a couple of Ambien that night and blacked out. I don't remember anything I did between 11:30 that night until the next morning." I spared my dad the details of the drugged texting to Mateo, Luke, and Darnell.

"That explains it. Your mother wanted to send you a bouquet of flowers and I told her no, that you specifically asked for the cereal marshmallows." My dad laughed.

"And that explains all of the weird gifts from everyone else," I stated. Things were starting to make sense.

"What did they send you?"

"Aunt Jackie sent me dog socks and you know I don't have a dog. Freddy sent me a bag of unicorn farts. Julia sent me a single bag of tea. And Uncle Charlie sent me 12 pounds of cheese."

"Charlie probably sent you the cheese anyway without even knowing about the Amazon list." My dad chuckled about his eccentric older brother. Forever a bachelor, Uncle Charlie often went off the grid for a month at a time to fish in Lake Superior.

I talked to my parents for ten more minutes and then got dressed in a Friars t-shirt and running shorts. A nice long walk on a brisk August morning would do me some good.

Outside, Mrs. Patterson was tending to her vegetable garden. She wore a washed-out flowered nightgown that had probably been a bright pink twenty years ago. I shook my head, hoping I never dressed like that when I was 80. She unknowingly provided me with comic relief.

"Morning, deeyah." She waved to me.

"Morning, Mrs. Patterson."

She studied my attire. "Where are you going today?"

"Just taking a walk." I started to turn away from her, down the opposite end of the sidewalk.

"I used to walk everywhere," she said. "But now my knees are bad. My doctah says I need surgery, but I don't want to."

"Well, you should listen to your doctor." I bent down to tie my shoelace. "I have to go, Mrs. Patterson. Have a good day."

"You too, deeyah." She waved goodbye and turned to her prized vegetables. That reminded me to pick my own when I got back.

Talking to Mrs. Patterson sometimes drained my patience, but I was kind to her. She was a lonely old woman and enjoyed our brief conversations. I hoped to live that long.

I headed down the sidewalk, unsure of my destination. Most of the residential streets in our part of East Providence were built in a grid system so as long as I only made rights or lefts and didn't cross Broadway, I wouldn't get lost. Once I made a right on Mauran Avenue, I walked four blocks west. No cars were parked in front of the usually busy Elks because it was closed on Sundays. My dad used to belong to the Elks when my parents still lived here. I walked three more blocks to

Lyon Avenue and turned right onto it. A few cars passed me on Lyon as I wandered past manicured lawns and proud, but simple, brick ranch homes.

I made a right on Warren Avenue, walking by a mix of homes and storefronts: a stereo shop, a Portuguese restaurant, a barbershop, and a laundromat. Most of the establishments were closed for the morning but would soon be full of patrons with the Sunday afternoon crowd.

Rhode Islanders are a unique bunch. We took pride in calling our home state the Ocean State. Because of the tiny islands within the state border, it had the most oceanfront property in the nation, much to the protest of California and Alaska residents. The official name of our state is "State of Rhode Island and Providence Plantations". Many progressives had pushed to remove the last three words so that it didn't sound like a slave state.

We enjoyed our Dunkin' Donuts iced coffee year-round, regardless of the winter weather. Starbucks didn't have a fighting chance. As the top donut city in the United States, Providence had two dozen donut shops per hundred thousand people. I grew up with coffee milk, but when I temporarily moved to Philadelphia, no one had heard of the unique syrup. Only boneheaded barbarians used a straw. Our milk was delivered by Monroe's Dairy and we could find a Del's Lemonade truck on every street corner in the summer. We ate "stuffies" (quahog clams stuffed in the shell) and preferred our calamari "Rhode Island style"--breaded and doused in marinara and served with hot peppers. Of course, we preferred creamy clam chowder over red. Those heathens in Manhattan had no clue about soup.

Giving directions was a subject that should have been taught in school. Nobody in Providence knew street names and gave instructions by landmarks like Shaw's grocery stores and Cumberland Farms convenience stores, which everyone called "Cumby's".

Neighborhoods were distinct with Portuguese, Italian, and Irish. Many of them had their own social clubs and restaurants that had been around for as long as I could remember. Most people lived and died in Providence. My family was the exception, with many of my relatives all over the country. I was happy to experience another city but glad to be home.

CHAPTER 12

At 4:00, I changed into jeans and a white off-the-shoulder top and headed out the door to visit my grandpa. Even though it was my birthday, I didn't mind driving to him because, much to his protest, he was no longer allowed on the road. He lived two miles away on Benefit Street, a couple of blocks south of Brown University.

My grandparents bought the three-bedroom bungalow before I was born for less than $200,000, but now it was worth close to a million. My grandma had participated in the Providence Preservation Society's Festival of Historic Homes several times. She loved her gardens. After my grandma died a few years ago, my mom tried to push my grandpa to sell and move into a smaller place, but he had no intention of leaving his home.

To my good fortune, no other cars were around and I parked the Impala on the street. I pushed through the white picket fence gate and hopped up onto the small porch. The blue-sided home was built in 1750 and featured the original chimneys, but my grandparents had upgraded to gas heat and double-pane windows. The first Colonist owner's name was on a historical plaque to the left of the door frame. I rapped the front door knocker.

A few moments later, my grandpa opened the door. He wore brown slacks and a navy-blue golf shirt. His white hair had been freshly trimmed and wire-rimmed glasses perched on his nose. Eighty-two years had been kind to him.

"There's my favorite peanut buttah cup," he said and pulled me into his arms. "Happy birthday, Reese."

"Hi, Grandpa."

He shepherded me into the house.

We strolled into the kitchen, my sandals clacking on the authentic wide pine floors that had been refinished a few dozen times. We sat at the table, near

96

one of the early fireplaces that had since been closed off. I pulled my phone out of my back pocket and put it on the table.

"You know I could've come to you," Grandpa said. "I can take the bus. I'm not 90 you know."

"I know. But I already had plans to come to this end of town," I replied.

"Don't lie to me." He waved a wrinkled finger at me. "You can't get anything past your gramps."

I barked a laugh. Even though he was long retired and in the downhill of his life, he never failed to make me chuckle.

"What do you want to drink?" Grandpa asked me. He stood and grabbed two glasses out of his cabinets.

"Water is fine."

"What? Are you a child?" He turned and glared at me. "You need something strongah than that."

Before I could answer, he pulled a half-empty bottle of Jameson out of the cabinet.

"It's a Sunday afternoon," I protested.

"And?" Grandpa filled the glasses three-fingers full of the whiskey.

97

He set them on the table in front of me. "No sissy ice cubes for you. I'm gonna teach you how to drink your booze. You've been doing it wrong for years. It'll put hair on your chest."

"Ummm…" I glanced down at my obvious female chest.

Grandpa waved a dismissive hand at me. "That's okay. It'll put hair on *my* chest!"

He clinked his glass against mine and we drank up.

"Did I ever tell you that my grandpa taught me how to drink?" he asked.

"No."

"Gave me my first sip of whiskey when I was eight."

"No way." I shook my head, unconvinced.

"It's true. He said I needed to learn to be a man. He gave me one fingah full every week for a year. Said it would build up my tolahrance."

"Did it work?" I asked and took a sip.

"I don't know. You tell me." Grandpa threw back the rest of his drink in one gulp.

I howled in laughter.

"Wanna know something else about our family?" His bushy eyebrows waggled.

"Sure."

"My grandpa's grandpa bought a knife set from Paul Reverah. He was a silvahsmith, ya know."

"No way…"

"Would I lie to you?"

I cocked my head and studied him with suspicious eyes.

"He did. I sweayah. That's it right theyah." Grandpa pointed to a weathered six-inch knife mounted on the wall above the sink.

"That knife has been there as long as I can remember and you're just now telling me that it was bought from Paul Revere?" I raised a hand in protest. "I call B.S."

"It's a fact. I didn't want those old ladies from the Historical Society begging me for it," Grandpa said. "If a lady's begging me for something, it'll be for something better than a knife."

"Grandpa!"

"The ladies beg me for my chowdah recipe." He winked at me.

I shook my head and chuckled, knowing that he was joking with me. Or was he?

"You hungry?" he asked. "I ordahed pasta from Camille's and it'll be here soon. Nothing but the best for my granddaughtah's birthday."

Camille's. I hadn't eaten there since the night I met Darnell.

"Sounds great," I said.

"While we wait fahr it, I'll turn on Pandorah." He pulled his phone out of his pocket and tapped it.

"How do you know about Pandora?" I asked as vintage music filled the room.

"Do you think I just fell off the turnip truck?" Grandpa glared at me in righteous indignation.

"I don't even know what that means."

He laughed and shook his head.

"Do you know who's singing this?"

I listened hard to the big band sound. "Sounds familiar."

"You youngins have no idea about Frank Sinahtrah, do you?"

"Who's that?"

Grandpa slapped a hand to his forehead, knocking his glasses askew on his nose.

"I'm joking!" I laughed. "Of course, I know Frank Sinatra. Mom constantly played him. She said you taught her all about him."

Grandpa fixed his glasses and chuckled. "You got me."

"I learned from the best between you and Dad."

"This is fun. We should make this a regulah thing. What are you doing next weekend?"

"I don't know. Haven't planned that far ahead." If Mateo, Luke, or even Darnell asked me out, they would have to wait. Grandpa trumped them. No matter what.

"I'm dancing at the community centah on Saturday. You should come with me."

"Ummm... Dancing with a bunch of old people?" I gawked at him like he was trying to force-feed me liver.

"You'll have a good time. I promise. Would I steerah you wrong?"

"You mean like when I was a kid and asked for a ham sandwich and you took my palms and buttered them and told me I could have a *hand* sandwich."

"I think we need more whiskey!" Grandpa chuckled, avoiding his guilt. He poured himself another three fingers full and leveled mine off. Since I was driving home in a few hours, I couldn't drink much more.

"Because you're buying dinner tonight, I can make us dinner next weekend before we go."

"Deal." Grandpa clinked my glass again and finished half of his whiskey.

My phone buzzed on the table with a text, interrupting us. I glanced at the preview: Happy Birthday Reese.

From Darnell.

I thanked him for the birthday wishes and didn't hear from him again.

CHAPTER 13

The next morning, my face was still warm as I got dressed for work. Was it from Darnell wishing me a happy birthday or all of the whiskey that I drank at Grandpa's? Maybe a combination of the two. I still couldn't believe that Darnell remembered to text me on my birthday. Before last night, I hadn't had any contact with him in several days when he left me hanging on my last text to him. His hit-or-miss texts confused me, but I also knew he wasn't one to play games.

The entire time we dated, he was clear about his feelings for me. I was the dumbass who wouldn't commit. He'd often buy me flowers for no reason, tell me how beautiful I looked (even when I came back from a run), made me his delicious homemade chicken noodle soup when I was down and out with the flu, and helped me build my garden.

Maybe now he was testing the waters with me. Touché, Darnell, touché. Maybe he didn't want to get too close to me in case I rejected him again. If I was him, I'd keep my protective distance, too. I wasn't sure how to approach him without scaring him off. But then again, he did wish me a happy birthday. Unlike Luke and Mateo.

When I walked into work, Jenna met me with a broad grin.

"Mornin' birthday girl," she said. "How are you feelin'?"

"Better than yesterday morning, that's for sure."

"Good. How did you spend the rest of your weekend?"

"I talked to my parents and my dad filled me in on the mystery of the cereal marshmallows."

"What did he say?"

"That I asked for them on my Amazon wish list."

Jenna laughed so hard that she knocked a few pens off of her desk.

"Another fallout from the Ambien walrus," I said.

"That's hilarious," Jenna sputtered, coming down off the high of her laughing fit.

"Then I had dinner last night with my grandpa and I offered to make dinner for him this Saturday."

"You did what? Girl, you don't cook." Jenna twirled the pink strand of hair in her fingers. "The last time you cooked, you made burned spaghetti. I mean, how hard is it to make spaghetti?"

Jenna was right. What was I thinking?

"I can't order take out, because he'll know I didn't cook it. He's smarter than that."

"What are you goin' to do?"

"I have no idea."

Between reviewing documents over the next few hours, I googled so-called easy recipes. My mind went dizzy at a half teaspoon of this and a pinch of that. How much was a pinch? What was the difference between a crockpot and a stockpot? How would I zest a lemon? What did it mean to rest something? Take a nap? I wasn't even sure if I owned any spices other than salt and pepper. How ironic that I had a garden and didn't cook. Most of my fresh produce went to my grateful co-workers and neighbors with a note "Free to a good home".

By the end of the day, I still hadn't figured out what I was making for my grandpa. I swallowed my pride and texted the one person who I hoped could help me. I was desperate and would endure the possible fallout.

I chewed my lower lip and wrote: Hi! I need your help. Plz :)

What's up? Darnell texted a few minutes later.

I promised to cook dinner for my Grandpa on Saturday, I wrote.

Darnell texted: But you don't cook. I always cooked for us.

Thanks for stating the obvious, Darnell. If he could only see me rolling my eyes.

Can you help me figure something out? You're the best chef I know, I wrote, hoping flattery would help my case. Darnell had graduated from Beacon Charter School for the Arts in Woonsocket. He was top of his culinary arts program and then received a full scholarship to Johnson and Wales. That's how the head chef at Camille's found him.

A few minutes passed and I panicked assuming that Darnell was thinking of a way to let me down gently. He could probably see right through me.

You free Wednesday? he finally texted.

I exhaled and quickly checked my calendar. Yes.

Meet me at the community garden in Mt Hope at 6, Darnell wrote. Knowles St by Billy Taylor Playground.

Billy Taylor was a local, urban hero. Born with a heart condition in 1956, Billy Taylor was the eighth of sixteen children. He graduated from Rhode Island College and then established the Pleasant Street Peasants. This group showed the Mount Hope urban youth that another world existed outside of the 12 blocks that most of the youth would never see beyond by taking them to museums, movies, and camping trips. When Billy Taylor died at 29, the park on Camp Street was named after him.

How will this help me cook for Saturday? I texted.

Just be there.

CHAPTER 14

On Wednesday after work, I dodged in and out
of traffic to race home. I had forgotten to bring a change
of clothes and didn't want to show up at the community
garden in heels and a dress. After I changed, I left my
house at 5:30 and headed to the north end of town
where the garden was through Wayland and the
Freeman Plat Historic District. I could have gone around
the west side on I-95, but rush hour traffic was hit or
miss. I didn't want to make Darnell wait since he was
doing me a huge favor.

At 5:55, I parked my big car in the shade of
maple trees along Knowles Street. Over the vine-
covered chain-link fence, I could see the tips of Darnell's

hair and a red bandana around his head. He bobbed his head up and down as if he was talking to someone but I couldn't see anyone else. Glad that I changed into my Chuck Taylor's, I walked through the grass to the gate on the right side toward the big blue sign that said *Mount Hope Community Garden.*

As I pushed the chain-link gate open, I discovered what Darnell was doing. He was chatting with a group of kids, worn garden tools in their hands, ready to dig up the earth. He glanced up at me, mentioned to the kids that he'd be right back, and sauntered over to me.

"Hi, glad you could make it," Darnell said. He hugged and kissed me on the cheek, despite the 'eew gross' mockery from the gawking kids. He wore a grey J&W alumni t-shirt full of dirt stains, tattered shorts, and work boots. A few flecks of dirt took up camp in his beard. I wasn't dressed as grungy as him, but I was glad I changed out of my work clothes.

"Thanks for helping me." I glanced around to the chattering kids who probably wondered who I was. "What are you doing here?"

"I work here," Darnell said. "Well, it's not technically work. I volunteer. Started last summer when I found out this garden would be shut down because no one stepped up to run it. The kids are here to learn how to garden and cook with the food we grow."

"No kidding." I was in awe of his selflessness. "How did I not know this?"

"I dunno." Darnell sheepishly grinned. "It's not something I post on Instagram."

"You should. This is so amazing," I gushed. "Does your head chef at Camille's know about the good work you're doing?"

"Probably not. Since I don't work there anymore."

I threw up my hands. "What? Why didn't you tell me?" Because I was too absorbed in my own life to ask about his.

"I didn't think it was a big deal."

"Well, what are you doing now? I mean besides this?" I flicked a hand toward the flourishing tomato, pepper, onion, and broccoli plants surrounding us.

"I opened up a food truck last month called Farmfood," Darnell said. "I take some vegetables from here and the ones from my home garden and use them to make sliders, salads, and wraps with local organic food."

110

A scrawny youngster holding up a rotten tomato interrupted us. "What do I do with this?"

"Toss it into the compost area," Darnell directed him.

"Thanks, D-man." The boy ran off.

I chuckled.

Then Darnell turned back to me. "So, you said you needed some help?"

I was so mesmerized by the goodwill going on around me that I completely forgot why I came in the first place. Darnell's generosity and time with these kids were impressive. He would make a wonderful father. We could have had our own kids by now if I hadn't been so stupid. I wanted to be with him again but I feared he would reject me.

"Yeah, like I texted you," I explained, "I need to cook something for dinner for my grandpa on Saturday. Do you have any ideas?"

"You're welcome to take any of the vegetables here." Darnell swept his arm toward the gardens around us.

"Yeah, but I don't know what to do with them," I protested with hands on my hips. "Will you please help me? I promise to make it up to you."

Darnell laughed out loud. "I tried to teach you so many times. Good thing you're cute."

I blushed. Darnell's kitchen prowess made me look like I had botched surgery on an innocent vegetable. If the kitchen police ever knocked on my door, they'd see red splattered walls and arrest me for the murder of a tomato.

"Come with me. I'm sure you have some tomatoes and peppers from your garden, right?" Darnell walked through the maze of lush green plants, pointing out Roma tomatoes and jalapeno peppers.

"Yes." I followed on his heels.

He stopped at a bed full of green herbs and pointed to them. "What about cilantro and parsley? And basil?"

I shook my head. He bent down and yanked a few stems of each out of the rich earth and handed them to me. I followed him to the next cluster of plants.

"How about onions and garlic?"

"Nope."

Darnell again pulled a few of the plants out of the ground and held them out for me. As he was bent over, I couldn't help but focus on his toned butt. I had to stop myself from licking my lips in front of the neighborhood kids. If Darnell only knew how hot he was.

I added the onions and garlic to the pile in my hands. "Now that I have all of this, what am I doing with it all? Will you help me cook it?"

Darnell chuckled and clapped his dirty hands together, knocking specks of dirt to the ground. "What's it worth to you?"

"Um, I--" I started to say. "Anything you want."

"I'm joking!" Darnell laughed. "You know I love to cook. I'll sous vide some chicken and sauté the veggies in a grill pan for you."

"Who is Sue Veed? Your friend?" I wondered out loud.

"Reese…" Darnell shook his head and chuckled at me. His mouth turned up into a cute grin. "No, sous vide is a way to cook meat or even eggs in a hot water bath. It's a French thing."

Darnell's cuteness factor went up again. Speaking of French… what I wouldn't do to French kiss him again. God, I was such an idiot to break up with him. With the kids around, I had to cool my libido if I wasn't careful. Darnell was smart, soft-spoken, kind, patient with me, good with kids, and, even in his grungy clothes, he was hot. I had to redeem myself if I ever had another chance with him.

I followed Darnell through a few more patches of vegetables and herbs as he checked on his students' progress. A group of them knelt in the dirt, digging with old hand tools and pulling weeds.

The boy who previously held the rotten tomato snickered at us.

"Hey D-Man, who's your girlfriend? She's got some O.G. kicks." The lanky youngster nodded to me and then back to Darnell. "You stiffing us?"

"This is Reese." Darnell motioned to me. "And she's not my girlfriend. Chill." He rolled his eyes.

I cringed and turned away, hoping that Darnell didn't catch my cower. Kids had a way of talking without a filter.

Fifteen minutes later, I left the community garden with an armful of fresh vegetables and herbs. Darnell gave me quick instructions on how to keep them fresh for the next few days until he could come over and cook with me on Saturday.

I had to come up with a way to thank him.

CHAPTER 15

When I got home at 7:00, crickets warmed up for their evening symphony. Mrs. Patterson was rocking on her porch like she was in a senior drag race.

"Hi, Reese." She waved to me. "What do you have, deeyah?"

"Just some fresh veggies for dinner on Saturday." I didn't want to stop and talk, for fear I might drop something. "I'll catch you later, Mrs. Patterson."

Inside, I set the produce on the kitchen counter and pulled my phone out of my bag.

I sent a text to Darnell: Thanks for your help today. I owe you. See you Saturday morning.

Since he was still at the garden, I didn't expect him to reply immediately. In the meantime, I needed something to eat.

I opened the fridge and found a few bottles of Sam Adams Summer Ale, a bag of baby carrots, an open container of onion dip, and the 12 pounds of cheese from my Uncle Charlie. What would I do with that much cheese? Two hundred grilled cheese sandwiches were not an option. If someone ever asked me why my fridge was so bare, I'd have to lie and say my power went out.

Where was a blueberry muffin when I needed one?

As I inspected the freezer, my phone buzzed on the counter with a text. I shut the door and stepped over to it.

A group text from Ebony to Val and me: Lunch tomorrow?

I'm in. Where and when? I wrote.

Me too, Val responded.

Union Station Brewery? Ebony texted.

Works for me. That's 5 mins from my office, I wrote.

116

C U then, Val replied.

I went back to my quest to find some dinner. My pantry was bare except for a couple of boxes of cereal, a can of tomato soup, and an almost empty jar of peanut butter. I didn't even have any bread. How pathetic was I? I put Mother Hubbard to shame. I would even mess up those home delivery meal kits with kindergarten instructions. *Worst Cooks in America* would love me. Whenever my friends hosted a dinner party, I was the token guest who brought a few bottles of wine because they knew I couldn't cook.

My stove terrified me. I was certain I would start a fire. My future husband would have to cook, otherwise, I, and our children, would starve. On the rare occasions that I assembled a salad, I proudly posted the jumbled bowl of greens on Instagram proving to my friends that I could make something, and not destroy the kitchen in the process.

Now the only solution was to go out. I grabbed my wallet and house keys and headed out the door. No need to bring my phone since it was a quick walk.

Two blocks later, I was at the entrance to Madeira Restaurant. I loved having a plethora of different restaurants within walking distance. Perfect for a non-cook like me. On the times that I didn't go out, Uber Eats offered me great suggestions with their algorithm based on my many previous orders. I had no shame that PieZoni was on my speed dial.

After consulting with the hostess over the menu, I ordered Galinha Em Molho De Alho - otherwise known as chicken in garlic sauce, served with rice and Portuguese fries. If only I could cook something like that and impress my friends. Good thing I was a runner, otherwise I'd weigh 500 pounds from eating out all of the time.

Twenty minutes later, I headed back home with a bag of steaming Portuguese cuisine.

Darnell had texted me while I was gone: Good to see you. Glad to help. See you Saturday :)

My cheeks warmed. Darnell always managed to make me smile. I didn't know why he was still single. Probably because stupid women like me didn't know what they had.

After decanting my takeout onto a plate (I couldn't cook but I wasn't a barbarian), I took my dinner into the family room and turned on the TV.

Summer television was worse than going to Target on a weekend. A Red Sox game. Not tonight. Some extreme mini-golf reality show. No thanks. Real Housewives of whatever city. Oh please no. A DIY show about selling a fixer upper. Eh, I already bought one. I finally settled on a mini marathon of *The Big Bang Theory*.

After a couple of hours of watching Leonard and Sheldon's antics with their friends, I called it a night. As I trudged up my steps to go to bed, my phone buzzed in my hand with a text.

You up?

From Mateo.

My nether regions immediately dampened in response. He gave me a lusty high right when I needed it. Mateo was my guaranteed ego boost and left me feeling satiated. Even though we didn't have much in common, he had a way of making me lose all rational thoughts and turning my body to mush. It was near-impossible saying no to him. Besides, I was not in a committed relationship, so I could have as much knock-around fun with him as I wanted.

Even though I thought about Darnell all the time, my hope could be in vain if we'd ever have a relationship again. But I was a woman and I still had needs - even if they were short-term with Mateo.

Yes, I replied.

Be there in 20, he wrote.

After my Portuguese dinner, I would satisfy my remaining Portuguese cravings with a helping of Mateo.

CHAPTER 16

The next day at 12:25, I cut through Biltmore Park to get to Union Station Brewery to meet Ebony and Val. Before I left the office, I had asked Jenna to join us but she had a deadline to meet and couldn't stop to eat. In the park, a few working stiffs sat at the wooden benches noshing on sandwiches and wraps. A handful of colorful bikes were chained to racks. In the small grassy quad, a young boy and his mother were trying in vain to fly a kite in the temperate breeze.

Cars whizzed past me on Exchange Terrace and I waited for a gap to make a break for it like a nervous squirrel. Ebony and Val sat at a black metal bistro table on the cement patio and waved me over. A pair of iced teas sweated on the table in front of them. After I hugged them and kissed their cheeks, I settled into the empty chair next to them.

Within minutes, a server approached and took our order. I opted for a glass of water and a wedge salad with shrimp while Ebony and Val wanted cauliflower tacos and Rhody calamari.

"I had the worst morning," Ebony moaned. As she leaned forward to take a sip of her tea, her long black braids dangled on the table. "I brought on a new football player this morning, and he put a hand on my leg during our meeting and told me he wanted to make me his biggest fan. Blech. Who *does* that?"

"I think you need something stronger than iced tea," I suggested. "We're at a brewery, after all."

"I would if I wasn't going back to work," Ebony said. "I need to be on my game later because I have a few clients to meet."

"What did you say to the guy anyway?" Val asked.

"First, I told him that if he ever laid a hand on me again, I wouldn't mind risking jail time," Ebony explained. "Then I told him to get the hell out and showed him the door. No ten-million-dollar contract is worth that."

"Good for you," I told her and clinked her glass with mine.

"Of course, the player made a scene when I kicked him out, blaming me. My boss came out of his office and heard the commotion. He was first annoyed that we lost the contract, but then I told him what happened and he held the door open for the jerk."

"You have a good boss," Val said. "I don't know if mine would do that. He's not a jerk like that player, but he has zero personality. When I talk to him, he says maybe three words and that's it. I don't know if it's me, or what."

"I'm sure it's not you," I said. "I've known you since we were five and you've never had a problem making friends. I remember our first-grade teacher putting the new kids with you because you made everyone feel at ease. You shared your crayons."

"I guess you're right," Val replied. "Maybe I just need a new job?"

The server came back with our lunch order and set the plates in front of us.

As I took a bite, a familiar face pushed through the entrance doors and headed our way. I smiled at him and motioned for him to stop at our table.

Luke.

"Hi, Reese," he said as he bent down and hugged me. He was dressed in a golf shirt and jeans, unlike his usual rugged boat wrapping attire. "Who are your friends?"

Even though Luke and I had dated, he hadn't met my friends. It was tough enough getting him to commit to a time with only me, let alone with anyone else.

"This is Ebony and Val." I gestured to the girls. "What are you doing here? Don't you work at the docks during the day?"

"I had to meet a client," Luke explained. "He was coming in from Newpaht and I figured I should dress up for the occasion. Didn't want him to think I was a bum." He raked a hand through his shaggy blonde locks.

"How'd it go?" Val asked.

"Eh." Luke shrugged. "I mean, I'll take the job because it pays well. But I can tell this guy'll be a pain."

"I was just telling the girls about a similar situation that I had this morning," Ebony chuckled.

124

"You look too nice to be a boat wrapper." Luke grinned at her for an extra-long moment.

Ebony smiled sheepishly, something I rarely saw her do. "Thank you."

"Well, I have to go," Luke spoke again. "It was good to meet you all. Reese, I'll talk to you later." And he was off.

"I wouldn't count on it," I chuckled under my breath as I took a bite of my salad.

"Why do you say that?" Val wanted to know.

"Because as nice as Luke is, he's a flake," I explained. "He takes hours, sometimes days, to answer a text. And that's if he answers at all. He and his roommates have folding chairs in their living room. They eat off paper plates too. And don't ever expect him to show up on time."

"He has a roommate at his age?" Val questioned.

"Two." I held up a couple of fingers.

Val grimaced, knowing that most people our age either lived on their own or with a spouse.

"Well, he seemed sweet to me," Ebony stated as she gazed in the direction where Luke wandered off.

"Girl, you're only saying that because he flirted with you," I said. "Don't let his good looks and charm fool you."

"After dealing with arrogant athletes all the time, he's like a breath of fresh air," Ebony explained. A goofy grin formed on her face.

Thirty minutes later, I headed back to work with a full stomach and was satisfied that I spent my lunch hour with my best friends.

* * * *

As I was heading out the door to go home, my phone buzzed with a text.

"Seriously?" I chuckled when I read it was from Luke.

Good to see u, he wrote. Ur friend Ebony is cute. Cool braids. Do u mind if I ask her out?

I smiled at Luke's unprecedented take-charge attitude. It was rare that he texted me first - and had a lot to say.

Good to see you too, I replied. Go ahead. She said you were sweet. Even though I had gone out with Luke a few times, I felt no jealousy that he was interested in Ebony. Good for them.

Cool. Can I have her digits? he texted.

I chuckled again that he replied within seconds. What had gotten into him? This wasn't the Luke that I knew and adored. But I did appreciate that he checked with me first before asking Ebony out. He could be a good boyfriend for someone. Just not for me.

CHAPTER 17

On Saturday morning, I awoke to a *tap-tap-tap* coming from the top part of my bedroom wall. Curious, I raked a hand through my bedhead hair.

"What the hell?" I sat up and watched the wall, waiting for something. But the sound stopped. I stood up and took a few paces toward the wall, staring at it. Owning an old house always kept me on my toes. One Saturday night while I was hosting a party, the electricity on my entire second floor went out leaving Val stranded in the dark in my upstairs bathroom. The electrician was kind enough to come on a Sunday and discovered that my wiring was set up like a bowl of spaghetti.

Tap-tap-tap. There it was again, but this time in the lower corner.

Bending down to examine the spot, I placed my hand along the wall but felt nothing except the plaster.

An instant later, a mouse scampered out of the small gap between the baseboard and the wall, ran along the floor and out of the room. I shrieked and jumped a foot back toward my bed. Normally, I wasn't afraid of mice, but this little guy startled me. Great. If there was one, a whole family of furry critters most likely lived in my rafters. Oh, the joy of living in an old house.

My phone rang on my bedside table and I snatched it up.

"Hi, Darnell," I said. My face warmed instantly. If he only knew that I was crushing on him again. But I had to take things slow.

"Will you be home in an hour?"

I quickly checked my phone clock. 9:15.

"Yeah. Why?"

"I can come over then to start cooking for you," Darnell said. "Did you put everything away like I told you?"

"Yes." I chuckled knowing that Darnell meant well for the non-cook in me. He would be right to

129

assume that I might put something in the freezer if he didn't tell me not to.

"Okay, great. I'll see you then." He hung up.

Crap. I had one hour to get ready, pick up any rogue laundry around the house, and look presentable for Darnell. I couldn't let him see my hair sticking out everywhere and chocolate stains on my sleep shirt. In the next 20 minutes, I took a shower, cursed a few times as I nicked myself shaving, then dressed in a blue tank top and white shorts.

I ran downstairs, folded the unkempt blanket on my couch, put some dirty glasses in the dishwasher that I found on the kitchen table, and wiped cookie crumbs from the counter into the trash can. I neatly stacked the magazines on my coffee table and cleaned the smudges on my fridge. Why was I so concerned? Darnell probably didn't care and had been to my place many times, but I wanted to make a good impression on him. Call it wishful housekeeping.

At 9:55, I ran back upstairs and blew dry my blonde hair. After the torture of the summer sun, I needed a good hair day. I wanted to look good but without Darnell thinking I tried. He wasn't one to hang around high-maintenance people. Especially women with three-inch nails who couldn't dig in the dirt with him.

Just as I put the hairdryer away and spritzed my head with some hairspray, my doorbell rang. I ran back down the stairs, almost falling on the last step. I reached for the railing to catch my balance. Accident averted.

I opened the door to Darnell holding a filled poly grocery bag in one hand and a cardboard cup carrier with two cups in the other hand. His black t-shirt and cargo shorts added to his cuteness factor. Two weeks had gone by since the last time he was on my porch.

"Hi," I said.

"Good morning. I brought you some iced coffee." Darnell leaned toward me and kissed me on the cheek. "Just cream, right?"

"Yes. I can't believe you remembered. Thank you." I took the cup carrier out of his hand and welcomed him inside. He followed me to my kitchen and I put our coffees on the counter. "You're not working at the food truck today?"

"Nah, my staff can open it up. I have some more important things I need to do," he said. "I'll get there for the dinner crowd."

131

I smiled hoping that he meant me, but I wasn't pushing it. Not yet. I pointed to his grocery bag. "What's in the bag?"

"My sous vide cooker and the chicken." Darnell pulled a foot-long black and silver three-inch wide cylinder out of his bag and set it on the table. He attached the accompanying cord and plugged it in. The black end of the cylinder lit up with blue digital numbers. "Do you have a stockpot?"

"You know I don't speak chef." I shrugged in confusion as if he was talking in a foreign language.

"Sorry," he said. "A large pot."

"In the lower cabinet." I pointed to the door next to the fridge. "Though I'm sure you'll want to wash it since I don't know the last time it was used. This morning I saw a mouse running around upstairs so who knows if it has critter droppings in it."

"Reese..." Darnell chuckled and shook his head. "What am I gonna do with you?" He pulled the pot out and laughed.

"What's so funny?" I stood with hands on my hips.

"There's a spider web in it," Darnell said.

"I have mice *and* spiders!" I shrieked.

132

"Don't worry, I'll protect you."

I was going to fall right off the cliff if he kept saying things like that.

Darnell immediately turned and washed the pot in the sink. I caught myself staring at his cute butt a few seconds longer than I should have. Good thing he couldn't see me ogling him.

Darnell then filled the pot with hot water and set it on the counter. He clamped the sous vide cooker to the inside of the pot and set the temperature.

"That looked really easy," I said.

He turned to me and grinned. "It won't bite. I'm sure you could handle something like this without burning down the kitchen.

"I don't know…"

"Baby steps," he said. "Now we start the chicken."

Darnell pulled two chicken breasts out of his bag, washed them down, and patted them dry. I watched him with boundless curiosity like I was getting the inside secrets from a gifted culinary magician. After seasoning the chicken with salt and pepper from my cabinet, he placed it in a large Ziploc bag. Then he washed his hands.

133

"Can you grab me the basil and parsley I gave to you the other day?"

"Sure." I efficiently plucked the herbs out of my fridge crisper drawer. "See? I did like you asked. I lined their baggie with a damp paper towel." I held the baggie up in between two fingers, posed for a moment as if wanting a kiss.

Darnell smirked and took the herbs from me. Quickly, he chopped them up on a cutting board. So much for a kiss. In an instant, the long stems were now tiny green pieces that he dropped in the chicken bag. He was a master with confidence and ease. No wonder the kids at the community garden loved him. I wondered if he enjoyed having this moment to show off his skills. Watching Darnell cook was so hot. His soft hands pressed against the plastic bag, hands that could have been pressing up against me. My mind wandered to other things he could have been doing to me.

As he dropped the bag of chicken into the waiting pot of hot water, he said, "This will cook for a few hours. You don't have to touch it. I already set the timer and it will turn off when it's done. When the timer dings, all you have to do is take it out of the bag and slice it up. Got it?"

134

"Aye-aye, Captain." I mock-saluted him. I wasn't going to beg him to banter with me, but at least he could react to my casual flirting. Maybe I was losing my touch?

Darnell's focus traveled to the corner counter where I had stacked a pile of freshly picked tomatoes and peppers from my garden. The onion and garlic from his garden were sitting next to them.

"Next, I'm making you some chutney to put on top of the chicken later." He grabbed the vegetables and chopped them into small chunks. I watched in amazement.

"Do you have ginger?"

"Is it red?"

"No, yellowy-brown."

"Nope."

"It didn't hurt to ask, so I brought some anyway." Darnell pulled a small baggie filled with multi-color spices from the bottom of his grocery bag. He pointed to it. "Ginger, paprika, cumin, and cloves."

"You're saying specific names but all I hear is spice, spice, and more spice."

He unzipped the baggie, took a step closer to me, and held it to my nose. My body instantly trembled with him that close to me. I wondered if he picked up on it.

"Smell. It's like the flavors of the gods," he said.

"Yum." A rich and hearty aroma filled my nose.

"I brought plenty so you can keep the extra for the next time I cook for you." He grinned at me.

Next time he cooks for me? I was looking forward to that. Was he also contemplating us getting back together? I could get used to Darnell's offerings. He was so kind to help me out. I owed him. Big time.

"You know, you're the first person who didn't make fun of me when I said I didn't know how to cook," I said.

"So, cooking's not your superpower. Big deal. You're better at other things."

"Like what?"

"Like making me feel good when I'm around you," he replied. "And I know my weaknesses. Thank you for not judging me."

"I try my best." I blushed.

"You're cute." Darnell quickly smiled at me and changed the subject. "Can you get me a medium pot with a lid to put this all in?" Sigh. I dropped my hook in the ocean but he wasn't taking the bait.

"Yes, of course." I would do just about anything for him. I grabbed a pot and lid from my cabinet and gave it a quick wash. My mom gave me the pot set as a Christmas present one year hoping I would escape from the dark side, but that didn't happen. Darnell scraped all of his choppings and half of the spices into the pot.

"Do you have sugar? It'll give it some sweet heat."

Mmm…. Darnell was another kind of sweet heat. I could stare at him all day.

"Now that I have." After I pushed a chair over for some added height, I plucked a small sugar bowl from an overhead shelf and placed it on the counter next to Darnell. He held it above the pot and poured a thin stream of sugar into the chutney mixture.

"You don't measure?" I asked, dumbfounded.

"Nope. I can gauge how much goes in by looking at it."

I blew out a low whistle. "I'm so jealous. I can't even make a grilled cheese sandwich without burning it and somehow the cheese is still hard on the inside."

"I know. Maybe you'll learn by osmosis?"

Darnell grinned at me and I blushed again. I could get lost in the chocolate pools of his eyes. Our eyes met and I did my best to hold his sparkly gaze for longer than a second. He broke the hold.

"We also need some whiskey," he said. "Do you have any?"

"My Grandpa would disown me if I didn't have whiskey in the house." I left Darnell in the kitchen and grabbed the half-empty bottle of Jameson from the liquor cabinet in the other room. I might not have food in my fridge, but by God, I will have Jameson! When I came back, I handed it to him.

"We don't need it yet," he explained, setting the bottle on the counter. "I want to let this chutney boil for a half-hour first before I add the booze." He put the lid on the pot and set the timer on my stove for 30 minutes. "In the meantime, we can clean up. Every good cook cleans up after himself. Or herself."

Wow, a man who cooks *and* does the dishes. I was smitten. Again.

Darnell filled my sink with water and dish soap and let the bubbles rise as he put his used magician's tools in the sink. He grabbed the faucet sprayer and, as soon as he pressed the old trigger button, it squirted water all over his shirt.

He jumped back at the sudden shower.

138

"My old house has decided to christen you!" I laughed out loud. "What did you do to upset the house? You used the sink just fine before."

"I know," Darnell chuckled as he held his hands broad. His soaked shirt sucked against the muscles in his chest. I couldn't help but stare at his toned body.

"Let me get you a towel to dry off with," I said after I picked my jaw up from the floor. The words came out of my mouth but my feet weren't moving. My brain had sent the message to my eyes to keep staring at Darnell. My feet would have to wait.

In an instant, Darnell lifted the wet shirt over his head and stood half-naked in front of me. I gaped at him and tried not to drool. Maybe my old house sprayed him on purpose so that I could see his bare chest? My feet might as well take a book out while they waited to move. Darnell's bare body put his shirt-covering to shame. I wanted to run my hands over every one of his muscles and trace his skin with my fingers. It had been over eighteen months since I last saw Darnell naked and I didn't remember him being so sexy. He must've started working out.

Then I noticed something new: a small script tattoo across his right peck. "What does *fortes fortuna adiuvat* mean?"

Darnell grinned at me and then glanced toward the ink. "Fortune favors the bold."

Indeed, it does.

"Do you like it?" he asked.

I continued to stare at Darnell's chest.

"Do you like it?" he repeated.

"Um, yes. Yes!" I couldn't believe I stuttered. Darnell must've thought I was a total idiot.

"I got it when I left Camille's and opened the food truck."

"It totally fits you." I wanted to run my fingers along the tattoo.

"You should come sometime."

"Yeah." I took an extra moment examining Darnell's chest.

"Can I have a towel now?"

"Oh, right. Sorry." My brain finally sent the message to my feet to move.

I left Darnell in the kitchen, ran upstairs to the linen closet, snatched a clean towel from the shelf, and hustled back down the steps. If I was thinking, I should

140

have asked him to come upstairs with me and get a sneak peek of my bed. In the kitchen, he exchanged the towel from me with his soaked shirt and wiped down his wet body. Naughty thoughts occupied my head, wishing that I was that towel.

"You don't happen to have a dry shirt that would fit me, do you?"

And cover that amazing body?

"I don't think so, but I'll put yours in the dryer."

"Well then I'll just have to stay like this," Darnell said. "I hope you don't mind."

Was he joking? I preferred it.

Shirtless, Darnell started washing my dishes. I grabbed a dishtowel, dried the items, and put them away. I liked that we worked as a team.

When we finished, he tilted the bottle of Jameson over the simmering chutney and long poured it. Again, he didn't measure.

"We'll let this cook for ten more minutes," Darnell explained, staring into my green eyes. "Then, we'll transfer it to a glass container to cool. When the chicken is done, you can pour the chutney on top and serve it to your grandpa."

"Thank you so much." I hugged him quickly. "I don't know how to thank you."

"I'm sure you'll think of something." Darnell winked at me and kissed me on the cheek. "I like grinders. All the way."

I laughed out loud. Of course. Darnell loved food.

CHAPTER 18

Darnell had left as soon as the dishes were done and I was alone in my house. A couple of hours later as I was sipping my iced coffee, my phone rang. It was Ebony.

"Hey, girl," I said.

"I had the best time with Luke last night," she said.

"That's awesome!"

"He's such a sweetheart. We went to The Eddy for drinks."

"I haven't been there. Where is it?"

"It's this cozy, dark bar downtown just off Westminster Street. We had a great time. Luke's a good

143

guy. So much better than those d-bag jocks. We talked for hours."

I hadn't seen Ebony this smitten in a long time, if ever. Maybe The Queen of Queens had a soft spot?

"Nice. I hope he didn't keep you waiting though."

"No, not at all. He was at the bar when I got there a few minutes early."

Luke? The same guy who kept me waiting a half-hour for a date? The same guy who took days to respond to a text? Was Ebony the reason that he was now a reformed flake? Feelings of inadequacy simmered through me.

"Wow, that's great. What did you two talk about?"

"Sports. He was fascinated with my job and knew all the ins and outs of different players. He was so easy to talk to. And quite the gentleman. He kissed me on the cheek at the end of the night and didn't once put out a creepy vibe."

"Good for you. Are you seeing him again?"

"Yeah, we're getting dinner tomorrow night."

Wow. Luke was on a roll. I hoped he maintained this new transformation for Ebony's sake. Or she would knock him into a corner and take no prisoners. He might surface with a broken nose if he pissed her off.

"That's cool. Where're you going?"

"To the Water Fire Festival and then dinner and drinks at CAV."

"Oooh, that sounds fun. I want to hear all about it."

"Deal. What are you doing tonight?"

"Having dinner with my grandpa and then going with him to the community center for dancing with his senior friends." I rolled my eyes at the last part.

"What's he making?"

"He's not. I am--."

"Girl, you don't cook!"

"Darnell came over this morning and helped me. Well, he did most of it. He made some chicken and chutney."

"Oooh, Darnell! That brother can cook for me anytime," Ebony sang. "How was he? Was it like a date?"

"No, I don't think so. But I did see a new tattoo on his chest. I'm telling you… he had abs like a Hershey bar."

"Wait, if it wasn't a date, how did you see his chest?"

I explained how Darnell soaked his shirt.

"Let me get this straight. He kisses you on the cheek every time he sees you, he came over and cooked for you, and stood half-naked in your kitchen. But it wasn't a date?"

"Yes."

I imagined Ebony wrinkling her nose and scratching her head.

"I don't know what he's thinking, but, Reese, you can't mess things up with him again."

"I'm trying not to!"

"No guy is doing all that if he doesn't at least have some interest in you."

"I hope you're right. I royally screwed up with him the first time around. I can't--won't--do that again. Promise me you'll help me avoid that."

"Deal," Ebony said. "He said he likes grinders, right?" Ebony asked.

"Yeah, why?"

"Get him a month's worth of sandwich rolls and all the fixings. All the way. That'll make him think of you for a while."

146

I chuckled at her over-the-top idea. "Maybe."

I hung up with Ebony and finished my coffee. She had a point. Doing something nice for Darnell might work to improve my chances with him again.

CHAPTER 19

After packing up the chicken and chutney, I drove it over to my grandpa's house for our dinner. Five minutes later, I parked in front, unloaded the food carriers from the Impala, and pushed through his gate.

With my hands full, I contemplated how I would use his door knocker.

"The one time he needs a doorbell," I muttered and shook my head.

With a foot, I knocked on his door and waited.

A few seconds later, Grandpa opened the door. "There's my favorite peanut buttah cup." He eyed my full hands. "Let me help you." He transferred the food carriers from my hands to his and held the door open for me with his back.

"Thanks, Grandpa." I kissed him on the cheek. He needed a shave.

We entered his kitchen and he set the food on the counter. "Which one of the boys do you want today?"

"Huh?" How did Grandpa know that I had all these men in my life?

"You know… Johnnie, Jack, or Jim?"

I chuckled at his whiskey joke. "I don't care. Whatever you find first."

Grandpa stepped away from me and headed to his liquor cabinet. "Johnnie is entertaining us tonight," he said as he pulled out a bottle of Johnnie Walker Blue.

"That's the good stuff! What are we celebrating?"

"We're celebrating that my granddaughtah cooked." He filled a couple of glasses three fingers high.

I turned away, hopeful that my Judas face didn't give me away. I unpacked dinner from the containers, grabbed two plates from the cabinet, and set them on the counter.

Grandpa handed me a tumbler of whiskey and clinked his glass against mine.

149

"Cheers," he said. "You ready to dance tonight?" He gestured to my pale-yellow sundress.

"I wouldn't miss it."

"Good, because we'll have fun," he said. "And there's an open bah."

"If I didn't know any better, I'd think you have a drinking problem," I teased.

"I don't drink any more than I did a year ago." Grandpa took a long sip of his whiskey. "I don't drink any less eithah."

I laughed out loud.

"You ready to eat?" I served us both a heaping serving of chicken and chutney.

"Wait, don't we need to heat it up?" he asked.

"Yes, you're--

Before I could finish my sentence, Grandpa whisked the plates away, set them inside his oven, and turned it on.

"Those plates can go in the oven?" I asked.

"I turned it on warm. They're fine. In the meantime, let's drink." He downed the rest of his whiskey and poured some more.

"Good thing I'm driving," I chuckled.

"I'm fine to drive. You just won't let me." Grandpa pointed a wrinkled finger at me.

"Me and the state of Rhode Island." I winked at him.

"I get in one fender-bender and your mother reads me the Riot Act," he moaned.

"Think of it this way," I explained, "when I drive you around town, we get to spend time together."

"True. I love spending time with my granddaughtah."

A few minutes later, Grandpa pulled the warm dishes out of the oven and set them on his kitchen table alongside our glasses of whiskey. I grabbed silverware from his drawer and took a seat next to him.

He put a forkful of chicken and chutney in his mouth. "This is wicked good!"

"Thank you."

"When did you learn to cook? The last time you cooked you lit rice on fahr and melted a plastic cutting boahd to the stovetop." He took another bite.

I covered my crimson face with a hand.

Grandpa continued, "And before that, we could have used your baked potatahs as hahckey pucks."

"I have to confess--"

"That you didn't actually cook this amazing chicken?" Grandpa raised a bushy white eyebrow at me.

"No." I shook my head. "Darnell did."

"Dahnell? Wasn't he the young man you dated a while back? I didn't know you were still in touch with him."

"It's a long story," I chuckled.

"Reese, I perfected the long story." Grandpa cleaned his glasses with his sleeve. "And you can't get anything past your gramps."

I relayed the short story of how Darnell showed up at my house two weeks earlier and that I begged him to help me cook dinner. He didn't need to know about Mateo or Luke or the Ambien Walrus. At least not yet.

"Sounds like you and Dahnell have some unfinished business." Grandpa rubbed his chin with a strong hand that had spent many years remodeling his house.

"It's complicated."

Grandpa rolled his eyes at me. "That sounds like a cop-out to me."

"It is." I frowned. "I should never have broken up with him. He's an amazing guy and I was too stupid to see it."

152

"Do you want to date him again?"

"Yes." I stared directly into Grandpa's eyes.

"Do you see yourself marrying Dahnell? Don't waste his time again if you can't answer yes to that." Grandpa's grey eyes bore into me.

"Yes."

Marriage. I hadn't thought about that kind of commitment until now. I liked being single and having options. Mateo was an ego boost. Luke might no longer be available now that he was chilling with Ebony. I hadn't been on Tinder in a couple of weeks, so I was sure more men were out there. On the other hand, dating was an exhausting part-time job. I had to keep track of everyone and make a deal with the devil that I didn't call someone by the wrong name. Being with someone for the rest of my life now sounded appealing. But it had to be the right person. Maybe it was Darnell.

"I don't even know if Darnell will give me a second chance."

"You can't sit inside your house all day and let your fears control your life. Believe me, I know. I didn't get to be 82 without taking chances."

"I think you made some sort of Faustian bargain." I pointed my fork at him. "I see people ten years younger than you who don't get around as well as you."

"Maybe it's all the drinking?" Grandpa winked at me and took another long swig.

His insights made me ponder as I pushed a strand of blonde hair out of my face. Had I been hiding inside the comfort of my house and not taking any real chances? Had I been coasting through life and not planning for my future? Would I wake up in ten years when I turned 40 and question what I had done with my life and who I spent it with? Did I want to leave a legacy or would my family tree end with me? If I didn't have kids, I wouldn't have grandkids to joke around with like I did with my grandpa. I definitely wanted that.

CHAPTER 20

After Grandpa and I finished Darnell's chicken, we cleaned the dishes. I waited in the kitchen while he escaped to his bedroom to change his clothes.

I studied the alleged Paul Revere's knife mounted above the sink as I pondered what my grandpa said. For as many jokes as he told, was he right about Darnell? But what if Darnell didn't have the same feelings towards me anymore? He had casually flirted with me a few times that morning. But what if I was imagining everything? What if Darnell was merely being kind by cooking for me? He was a nice guy. No one could deny that. But what if he wanted the same thing I did? I couldn't pass up that chance again.

155

Grandpa stepped into the kitchen and interrupted my thoughts.

"How do I look?" He now wore navy trousers, a starched white dress shirt that was unbuttoned at the neck, and black suspenders. His white hair was slicked up with gel and his glasses were freshly cleaned. He had shaved and a whiff of musty cologne lingered around him.

"I think the ladies will be all over you," I jested.

"That's the plan." He winked at me.

My phone buzzed with a text from Mateo.

Drinks tonight?

"Let me answer this real quick," I told Grandpa as I tapped my phone.

"Make it quick," he teased with an upward curve of his mouth. "We have a date."

Can't, I responded to Mateo. I have plans with my grandpa. Some other time.

K, Mateo replied.

As much as a hot night with Mateo sounded appealing, my grandpa came first. Always.

A few minutes later, Grandpa and I settled in the Impala. Much to his protest, I insisted that he get in the

156

passenger side. The seat springs squeaked as he sat down.

"This old girl still handling well for ya?" Grandpa tapped the interior side panel of the car, grazing his fingers along the waffle pattern.

"Yes, despite my mechanic saying she's on her last legs," I said. "But he's been saying that for a few years now."

"She's a tough old broad. Just like your grandma was."

"Yes, she is." I cranked open my window and Grandpa did the same. "Where are we headed?"

"Just go up Benefit Street." He flicked a hand in front of us. "I'll tell you where to turn."

We puttered down the tree-lined street, passing a showcase of Georgian mansions and Federal-style modest homes. My engine gurgled a few times, but the old car wouldn't give up.

"Turn on your blinkah and hang a right at the Eliza Wahd House," Grandpa instructed.

"Huh? Even though I grew up around here, I have no idea where that is," I chuckled. "I bet tourists get lost all the time if locals like you give them directions."

Grandpa laughed because he knew I was right. But that's how Rhode Islanders were. They couldn't give good directions if their lives depended on it. No one knew what the actual street names were, only the nearby buildings. Google Map drivers were wasting their time.

"I mean take the next right on Geohge Street."

I did as directed and turned at the historic Eliza Ward House onto George Street.

"Now make a left at the Rockefellah Library--I mean on Prospect Street." Grandpa smirked at me. "Then go past the Brown Green and make a quick right onto Watahman."

I turned right on Waterman and drove by Brown University's visitor center. "You taking me on the scenic route?"

Grandpa laughed. "Turn left on Brown Street and stay on that until I tell you."

I drove us along several blocks of residential homes, passing kids on bicycles and homeowners tending to their prized gardens.

"Make a right on Bahnes and the first left on Hope," Grandpa said. "At least I think that's what it's called."

As instructed, I turned right onto Barnes Street.

"I came up this way to go to Darnell's community garden." I recognized the more urban housing and patched streets. Houses were closer together and stop lights flickered at every intersection. Would he be there working with the kids even though it wasn't a Wednesday? My insides warmed at the thought.

"Go to the streetlight and hang a left and it's right theyah," Grandpa directed.

The community center parking lot was packed. Once I found an empty spot, we walked to the double-door entrance of the modest tan building. Inside, we roamed the hallway, passing a bulletin board on the wall filled with colorful posters announcing a chicken BBQ, a Labor Day picnic, and a movie night in the park. Board games were stacked on a nearby metal shelf.

In the multi-purpose room, music blared from a DJ table as couples cavorted on the dance floor. A lot of the men wore shirts and ties while the women wore dresses. Several large round tables lined the perimeter of the room and a makeshift bar served cocktails in the corner.

"Wow, this is great," I exclaimed, wide-eyed.

"I told you," Grandpa said.

159

An older woman wearing a blue dress and black pumps approached us.

"Hi, Robert," she said to my grandpa and flicked a wave at him. Multiple gold rings filled her fingers.

"How ya been, Dorahthy?"

"Just fine," Dorothy said. "Save me a dance later?"

"I wouldn't miss it." He blew her a kiss and she flounced off.

"Grandpa!" I shrieked when Dorothy was out of range. But then again, since she was older, maybe she couldn't hear very well.

"What?" He feigned innocence with a shrug and a sly smile. "What can I say? She likes me now that I gave her my chowdah recipe."

Before I could utter another word, a second woman came up to us. She wore a red dress and her grey and black hair was pulled up into a tidy nest of cornrows on her head.

"Hello, Robert. You're looking *fine* tonight," her sultry voice practically sang akin to Lana Del Ray.

I could have sworn she batted her eyes at him.

"Hello, Chandra."

160

"Who's with you tonight?" Chandra nodded toward me.

"This is my granddaughtah Reese," Grandpa said.

"Pleased to meet you, Reese." Chandra extended her three-inch manicured fingernails toward me. The hot pink color stood out against her dark skin. Thick, gold hoops hung from her ears, nearly grazing her shoulders.

"You too," I replied.

"You can call me Ms. Chandra," she said. "I love your dress."

"Thank you."

"I hate to be rude but I need to go," Ms. Chandra said to my grandpa. "Harry is waiting for me to dance with him. There is a space on my dance card if you want it."

"I'll gladly take it," Grandpa said. He winked at her.

Chandra left us, wandered into the middle of the dance floor, and found Harry.

"You gave her your chowder recipe too, didn't you?" I teased Grandpa.

"Yeah, but you're at the tops of my dance card."
He grabbed my hand. "Let's go."

Grandpa led me to the dance floor and stood
facing me. I had gone to clubs in Philly while in college,
did some impromptu dancing with the girls, and watched
a few episodes of *Dancing with the Stars*, but no one
had formally taught me any moves.

"Keep your chin up and mirrah me," Grandpa
said.

"Then how am I supposed to see what your feet
do?" I questioned.

"Don't worry. They'll move on their own."

He put all of his weight on his right foot and
lightly hopped. "This is the Lindy Hop, so rock-step. Do it
with your left foot." I did as instructed, hoping I didn't
look like an idiot. He shifted his weight to his other foot.
"Now transfah your weight and hold. Then walk two
times in place." His body was automatic as he spoke.
"Then hop back again. One-two-three-four-five-six-
seven-eight. Got it?"

I shook my head in confusion.

"Don't worry, it'll come." Grandpa took my hands
and moved my body congruently with his. I stumbled a
few times, but he caught me and we kept going. We

162

danced to songs by Ray Charles, Ella Fitzgerald, Lionel Hampton, and The Brian Setzer Orchestra. I missed a few steps but didn't let it stop me from having a good time.

"Are you having fun?" Grandpa asked me.

"Yes! How did you learn to move like that? I never knew."

"I grew up dancing and that's what we did," Grandpa said. "We'd go to dance halls every weekend. We did The Twist, The Stroll, and the Watusi."

"What's a Watusi? I asked.

Grandpa laughed out loud.

"Are you ready for a break? Get a drink?" He produced a handkerchief from his pocket and dabbed the sweat beads on his forehead.

"That'd be great."

Grandpa led me from the dance floor and we headed to the bar in the corner of the room. He held a hand up for me to place my order first.

"I'll take a vodka with cranberry but make it heavy on the cranberry since I'm driving," I told the bartender.

"Coming up." He motioned to Grandpa. "And you?"

163

"What kind of whiskey do you have?" Grandpa asked.

"Jack Daniels and Jim Beam."

"I'll take a Jack."

"A Jack and what?"

"Nothing. Just a Jack."

The young bartender glared at Grandpa like he had three heads. "Okay...."

Grandpa turned to me and muttered, "Amateur."

I choked on a laugh.

As we sipped our drinks, Dorothy strutted up to us, her hips sashaying back and forth.

"Hey Robert, you ready for that dance?" she cooed.

"Of course."

He faced me. "You okay by yourself for a little while?"

"Sure. I'll be fine. Go have fun." I motioned toward the middle of the room where dozens of senior couples lindied and jived.

Grandpa emptied his glass and set it on the bar, then escorted Dorothy to the dance floor.

"Reese!" A sultry female voice called from behind me.

Before I could answer, Ms. Chandra came around my side and stood in front of me. She held a manicured hand against her voluptuous hip.

"How you doin' tonight, baby?"

"Good, thank you."

"I saw you dancing. Didn't want you to feel left out. There are a lot of cute fellas out there--including Robert." She glanced over at my grandpa dancing with Dorothy.

"I don't mind." I smiled and scanned the room over her shoulder. "My grandpa's fun."

"Yes, he is. But I know someone closer to your age." She peered past me and grinned. "And here he is now with my drink."

She reached for a glass of wine that was presented to her.

"I'd like you to meet my nephew." Ms. Chandra beamed with pride and she herded him even closer to us.

Darnell.

CHAPTER 21

Darnell and I chuckled at the serendipity.

"I'll let you two get acquainted," Ms. Chandra giggled. She wandered off to the dance floor and left us by ourselves.

"Ms. Chandra is your aunt?" I asked Darnell, taking a sip of my drink.

"Well, great-aunt," he answered. "But don't tell her I said that. She likes to tell people she is a lot younger than she is."

I laughed at her own Faustian bargain. No wonder she and my grandpa got along so well.

"How did your grandpa like the chicken and chutney?" Darnell asked.

166

"He loved it. Had two servings."

"Good, I'm glad." Darnell smiled a wide, perfect grin. God, he was cute.

"But he found me out because he knew I didn't cook it." I recoiled. "I confessed and told him that you did it. The pressure was too much for me. I couldn't live a lie."

Darnell cackled heartily. I loved that I could make him laugh. He pushed a stray lock of hair out of my face. My face burned instantly.

Instinctively, I curled the hem of my dress in my fingers. Why was I nervous around him all of a sudden?

"You look good tonight," Darnell said, eyeing me up and down. He wore a black button-down shirt and black trousers that complemented his dark skin. He was a beautifully sculpted Adonis with shades of night. I hadn't seen him dressed up like this in a long time.

"Thanks. Uh, thank you." My breath caught as my cheeks flushed through my nerves. Warmth spread throughout me, down my spine to my toes. Yes, Darnell had been in my house earlier that morning, but I was sidetracked by his cooking prowess and didn't think about being alone with him. Now, my tongue betrayed

167

me as everyone in the community center seemed to fade away and the music softened in my ears.

"Listen, I have to go," Darnell spoke softly. He cocked his head toward the empty doorway.

"Will I see you later?" I asked. "Maybe we could get a cup of coffee or something? I still owe you for cooking for me."

"I don't think so."

Ouch.

"Oh. Okay," was all I could utter.

"See ya." Darnell flicked a half-wave at me and headed toward the door, leaving me alone.

What just happened? Did I miss something? I thought Darnell and I were getting along. Our cute bantering had given me hope. He had easily agreed to cook for me. I went to his garden. He took his shirt off in my house. The next logical step was for us to go out on a date again. Seconds ago, he told me I looked good. He always kissed me on the cheek in the past two weeks when he greeted me. Oh, wait. He didn't this time.

I rubbed a hand along my face where Darnell's lips should have been.

Maybe he was simply being kind to me. Maybe everything was all in my head. Maybe he couldn't bring himself to be more than friends with me. Did he have a sixth sense that I was with Mateo a few days ago? Sometimes my lady parts made decisions without checking upstairs. If being with Darnell meant giving up Mateo, I would gladly do it. Mateo gave me a quick hit while Darnell was the real deal. But I wasn't even sure if I had the opportunity with Darnell anymore.

After I set my half-drank vodka cranberry on a nearby table, I plodded into the nearest hallway to throw myself a pity party. Finding an abandoned folding chair, I fell into it, my shoulders sinking. I spread my knees and dropped my lifeless arms between them. So much for being prim and proper in a dress. Now would be a good time for a cigarette. If only I smoked.

I had foolishly envisioned myself dating Darnell again, but that was now an unattainable fantasy. Like reaching 120 mph on an odometer then coming to a screeching halt.

Darnell had every right to reject me. He had a great life and I was merely a blip in his fruitful existence. I envied the way he carried himself. His quiet confidence set the bar for all men. He had no idea how handsome

169

he was. Or, if he did, he didn't care. He was smart, kind, caring, selfless, and made me feel good about myself without coming on too strong. He was one of the coolest people I had ever met. He was the whole package. Any woman would be lucky to have him. I was a jerk to end things with him two years ago because I didn't want to be tied down. After my bad breakup in Philadelphia, I had protected myself by not getting too close to anyone again. And lost Darnell in the process. Was that horrible relationship responsible for my self-sabotage?

I stared down at the floor, not focusing on anything.

"What're you doing out herah?" Grandpa's voice called to me from the end of the hallway.

I glanced up and offered him a weak smile as he walked closer to me. He would always be my number one fan.

"I messed up," I said. "Big time."

"Why? What happened?" He held a glass of whiskey. "I left you ten minutes ago and you were fine."

"Ms. Chandra saw me and introduced me to her nephew."

Grandpa lifted a white, bushy eyebrow over his glasses.

"Darnell." I rocked back and forth in the chair, still mad at myself.

"Oh. You need this more than me." Grandpa offered me his whiskey and I took a sip. "How did you mess up?"

"That's just it," I sighed. "I don't know. I thought he and I were getting along the past couple of weeks. And even this morning. Then, just now, when I asked him if he wanted to get a cup of coffee later, he said no and bolted as if I was a freak."

"Well, first of all, he's an idiot for turning you down." Grandpa twirled a lock of my blonde hair through his fingers. "You are one of the most beautiful girls in town."

"Aww, you're just saying that." I tried my best to smile at him. He always made me feel better.

"And you're wicked smaht and you know how to put people at ease." He grinned at me. "You're my favorite peanut buttah cup."

"Thanks, Grandpa. It stinks because I thought I was mature enough now to realize what I had with Darnell. Only he didn't want me."

"You really like him?"

"Yeah."

"More than anyone else?"

"Yeah."

Grandpa draped an arm around my shoulder. "I know it isn't what you hoped fahr, but you'll be okay. I know you will. You are strong and can get through it." He nodded toward the dance hall where we heard laughter and music. "Besides, there are plenty of old men in therah that would love to dance with a pretty young lady."

I tried to laugh but only a muffle came out.

"Let me tell ya something," he said, cupping my chin in his hand. "Despite all those ladies in theyah who want to dance with me, I only ever loved one woman."

"Grandma."

"Yep." A silly grin formed on his face and he stared into space. "She was the love of my life for nearly 60 years. She was spunky and wicked smaht. Like you. She could always make me laugh. I loved being around her. I always thought I'd die before her because she was so full of life. I try to keep busy so that I don't have to think about her too much. She made me weak in the knees and I could barely speak when I was around her. She probably thought I was a fool. Being married to her

172

was the best time of my life. If I could only have her back."

"I miss her too."

I wanted what my grandparents had. No more settling. No more Mr. Right Now. No more thinking it will eventually come. I was 30 years old and it was time for me to have a permanent relationship. I wanted someone I could spend the rest of my life with. I wanted someone who I could talk to from morning until night and not realize that a whole day had gone by. I wanted someone who would ask me hard questions and not be afraid of my answers. We would be a team and still know when to spend time together and when we needed time away. I wanted someone who adored me but I didn't want to take advantage of that love. I wanted someone where I could remember the exact moment where we met and everyone around us faded away, where I knew that my life would never be the same.

Was it asking too much if he was pure eye candy too?

CHAPTER 22

I spent the next day skulking around the house, not changing out of my pajamas nor bothering to brush my hair. The morning dishes were strewn across the kitchen counter and I had dropped several napkins on the floor without troubling myself to pick them up.

As I nibbled on a bowl of popcorn and pretended to watch an episode of *Friends*, the mouse from the previous morning scampered across my living room floor. She (I decided it was a girl) paused at the entrance to a small opening in the baseboard and stared at me. Her tiny, white hands curled together like she was considering something.

174

"You can stay here," I told her. "I don't mind. Just don't eat my food." I popped a handful of popcorn in my mouth.

She glared at me, unblinking as if she understood what I said. I could have sworn she gave me a quick nod, then she scurried off through the crack in the board.

Is this what my life had come to? Me having a single-sided conversation with a mouse?

I glanced out the window and found Mrs. Patterson tending to her garden. As long as I stayed out of sight, she wouldn't try to talk to me through the window. Normally, I didn't mind, but I wasn't up for it today.

My phone rang on the coffee table. It was Val.

After a few seconds, I finally picked it up. I was not in the mood to talk to anyone, but guilt pushed me to take Val's call.

"Hey girl," she said. "What are you doing the weekend after next?"

"Let me check… my lunch at the White House fell through and Michael B. Jordan canceled our date… so nothing."

175

"Ha-ha. Very funny. Aidan's birthday is coming up, so I wanted to get everyone together at the Pub for it. You, me, Ebony, Jenna, and some of Aidan's friends."

"Sure. I'd love to celebrate your hubby's birthday. I have 12 pounds of cheese and a Danny DeVito life-size cutout I can regift."

Val laughed. "I'll let you know next week what time we're heading out."

"Sounds good."

I hung up with Val. It would be almost two weeks before we'd go out. Hopefully, by then, I would be out of my funk.

* * * *

The next morning, I dragged myself into work. Jenna was not at her desk, so I quickly headed to mine. I knew she would listen because she was a good friend, but I hated to moan about something when I had no control over it. My rejection of Darnell would go away on its own. I was sure of it.

I wasn't in the mood to go out for lunch. As I slurped a lonely can of tomato soup at my desk, Jenna strolled by.

"There you are," she said. "I came by to see if you wanted to get lunch, but I guess not."

176

"Eh."

"What's wrong, darlin'?" The pink strand in her hair glistened under the overhead fluorescent lighting.

"My weekend sucked."

"What happened?"

I relayed the ups and downs of the weekend.

"You'll be better in a few days. Give it time. There are plenty of fish in the sea." She patted my arm in a sisterly fashion.

I half-laughed at Jenna's ill attempt to cheer me up.

"Are you going out for Aidan's birthday?" I asked her.

"Yup."

"Hopefully I'll be in a better mood by then."

"Probably sooner. I know you." She grinned at me, her optimism shining through.

I admired Jenna's optimism. She had a way of making people feel better, no matter what they were going through. She was one of the most spirited people I had ever met. One time, when we were out for lunch, we befriended a group of college girls who were on their way to Canada to do some backpacking and Jenna picked up their tab, despite the low funds in her bank account.

Jenna gestured to herself. "If I can get over being dumped by a gay man, you can get over being turned down for coffee."

She had a point. It was only an invitation for coffee. It was not like I had asked Darnell to marry me after being together for a while. Jenna was wise beyond her 25 years.

"You're absolutely right. I can't let one rejection ruin my life."

"Atta girl!" Jenna slapped the edge of my desk. "You'll be on another date in no time."

"I don't know about that," I replied. "But I'll try to have fun when we go out for Aidan's birthday. I promise."

An hour later, my phone buzzed with a text from Mateo.

U busy Thursday? he wrote.

No. What's up? I texted back. Anything was possible with Mateo.

I'm having a soft opening for my new gym if u wanna come at lunch.

Wouldn't miss it.

Bring ur friends.

Even though it wasn't a night of hot sex with Mateo, seeing him would lift my spirits.

CHAPTER 23

On Wednesday, after two days of gradually feeling better about myself, I bounded into work. Jenna greeted me as I walked in.

"What are you doing tomorrow?" I asked her.

She scanned the calendar on her monitor. "A few meetings in the morning, but that's it. Why?"

"Do you want to come with me to Mateo's new gym? He's having a soft opening tomorrow and he told me to bring my friends. "

"Sounds fun."

"Great. We can head over at lunch. It's a couple of blocks away."

180

I left Jenna and headed to my desk to start my day.

After hours of reading documents, making phone calls, and attending meetings, I needed some coffee. When I came back from the break room with a steaming cup, my phone lit up with a new text.

From Darnell.

Oh my god. I hadn't heard from him since he turned me down for coffee on Saturday night. I didn't expect to hear from him again.

`My food truck will be downtown this afternoon at Waterfront Park. Be great to see you.` He added a smiley face emoji.

Huh? This was the same guy who rejected me but now he was inviting me to come to his food truck. He wasn't into games--he wasn't that kind of guy--but why the complete change of heart? Only a few days had passed, but the tone of the text was 180 degrees from what happened at the community center. If I wanted any clarity, I had to go see him. Otherwise, the frustration would eat at me and I'd torture myself with too many unanswered questions like *What did he mean?* and *What is he thinking*?

181

I quickly checked my calendar. Meetings filled up most of my afternoon. I'd have to wait hours to figure out Darnell's vibe.

Sounds fun. Will you still be there after 4? My afternoon is crazy! I wrote. I couldn't let him suspect that I was freaking out. I couldn't even bring myself to add an emoji, hoping that he didn't pick up on my exasperation. Clearly, I needed more lessons in How Not to Freak Out About a Man. My current insecurities trumped my usual confidence.

Darnell texted back a few minutes later: Yep. Will be there until 8 tonight. Sorry you're having a rough day.

What did he mean by that last sentence? Surely, he felt bad that I was swamped, but did that mean he *cared*? Figuring out men was like playing chess. Each move they took could mean something toward a future step. Or one false move could result in checkmate. Game over.

I spent the next few hours buried under work, but thoughts of Darnell crept into my head. I wanted to see him but was worried that I was setting myself up for disappointment. Again. I hoped I looked good in my purple and white flowered top and grey trousers. The heeled sandals on my feet not only gave me height but an added scoop of confidence.

When I finished my last email at 4:05, I shut my computer down and stopped in the ladies' room for a quick primp before I headed out the door. Jenna was already gone and the reception area was quiet.

I exited our building and wandered east down Dorrance Street toward the river. Waterfront Park was on the opposite bank. Financial District commuters rushed past me on the sidewalk as cars rumbled along the street in stop-and-go traffic. I cut across Dyer Street into the manicured green space that spilled out on the west side of Providence River. Aromas of barbeque and French fries fluttered into the air.

The new curved pedestrian bridge that spanned the river stretched out in front of me like a wooden horizon. The Wana wood structure paid homage to Providence's maritime past, bringing together old-world character and warmth. Sun-seekers rested on the plank benches that lined the sides of the bridge. With their parents nearby, children played along the lower levels closer to the water. I strutted along the lumber bridge, my heels clacking in cadence.

I spotted Darnell's food truck in front of South Water Street on the east side of the river and headed toward it. *Farmfood* spelled out in big, green letters along the side of the truck. A dozen people waited in front of the truck to get something to eat. I joined the end of the line and studied the placard menu: mac and cheese beet salad, duck tacos, chickpea and cauliflower patties, and the regionally favored crab cake with garlic aioli and remoulade. A kaleidoscope of aromas filled the air.

A few minutes later, I approached the window and Darnell's co-worker acknowledged me with a wave. He wiped his hands on a well-used cloth.

"Hi! What can I get you?" He rested his palms on the metal counter that separated us.

"I'll take a crab cake."

"Good choice. Anything to drink?"

"Just a bottle of water."

He turned and called to the interior of the truck, "Darnell, I need a crab cake." Then he turned back to me. "That'll be $17.50."

I pulled a twenty out of my wallet and handed it to him. "Keep the change."

184

"Thank you. Hang out here and it'll be up in a few minutes. What's your name?"

"Reese." I leaned into the counter and whispered like I was telling a secret, "Any chance I can pay my compliments to the chef?"

"Sure." The man turned again and yelled to the back of the truck. "Hey Darnell, someone wants to talk to you."

As the crowd dissipated, I stepped to the end of the truck and waited for Darnell and my food.

Darnell opened the back door and smiled at me. "Hey there. Glad you could make it." He hugged me and kissed my cheek. That was the Darnell that I knew. His biceps peeked out under the sleeves of his green *Farmfood* t-shirt. A black bandana was wrapped around his head. He looked good, or *fine,* how Ebony liked to say it.

"You have a good crowd here today. You're a hit," I said.

"Yeah, I try." Darnell blushed. It was cute.

"It's Wednesday. Don't you work at the garden on Wednesdays?" I asked.

"The kids all had something at school this afternoon, so I'm here," he explained.

"Aren't you supposed to be cooking my crab cake?" I tapped a heel on the sidewalk, mocking impatience.

Darnell grinned broadly and cocked his head toward the truck. "I started it and the guys'll finish it."

I chewed my lip as I tried to come up with exactly what I wanted to say next. "So… I… wanted to...um… ask you…"

"Ask me what?" Darnell eyed me, a small smirk forming on his mouth.

I blew out a nervous sigh. Even if Darnell didn't give me the answer that I wanted, I would at least know I had the truth. "Ask you… about the other night."

"What about it?"

"Well, I-- I-- um..." I blew out another sigh then spit it all out. "I wanted to know why you blew me off for coffee so that I could pay you back for helping me with my grandpa."

Darnell glanced away from me and then back again. "I couldn't."

"Couldn't or wouldn't?"

"Okay, wouldn't."

I shook my head in confusion. "Why *wouldn't* you? I thought we had a good time on Saturday morning."

"We did." Darnell offered me a half-smile.

"I don't understand." I flicked a hand toward him. "If we did--"

Darnell took a step closer to me, cutting me off. "I have to know something."

"Anything."

"Who were the guys in your house a couple of weeks ago? Are you seeing them?"

"Not really."

"What does that mean? Not really?" He glowered at me, waiting for an answer. His brown eyes bore into me.

My insides screamed. I was so stupid! Even though I didn't think twice about going out with multiple men, Darnell did. He didn't want to be a second, or even third, choice. I wanted to tell him that he was my first choice. Luke was now more interested in Ebony and Mateo was a friend with benefits. But Darnell didn't want to hear about the benefits. I couldn't bring myself to tell him the truth because I didn't want him to think badly of me. For the first time, I was embarrassed by my actions.

187

Before I could respond, a voice called from the truck window. "Reese! Crab cake!"

CHAPTER 24

Without a word, Darnell climbed back inside the food truck.

God, I was such an idiot. He deserved so much better than me. I had always prided myself on being independent and in control of my love life. But now that I wanted Darnell, I hadn't thought about the repercussions.

Defeated, I shuffled over to retrieve my food. Even though it was Darnell's pride and joy, I had no appetite. I took the brown bag and walked away, dragging my feet down the sidewalk.

Ten long minutes later, I found my car in the parking garage and drove home, leaving the food bag

189

on the vinyl seat next to me. I couldn't bring myself to eat.

When I arrived home, Mrs. Patterson was outside hunched over, watering her flowers with a hose. She silently reminded me that I needed to check for new veggies in my garden. But I didn't feel like doing it. The local bunnies would have a feast on me.

"Hello, deeyah." She waved to me. "How was your day?"

The worst.

"Fine," I lied. I glanced at the bag of food in my hands. "I have a crab cake here and I'm not hungry. Do you want it?"

"You sure you don't want it, deeyah?" She stood upright as much as her old bones would allow, changing the position of the nozzle and letting the hose water the grass.

"I'm sure." I stepped closer to her and offered the bag. "It'll go bad by tomorrow."

"Thank you. Better than my frozen dinner from the senior center."

I forced out a polite chuckle.

Inside my house, I found a bottle of red wine and poured a glass. I settled on the couch and kicked off my heels. So much for the added confidence. Now that I knew why Darnell turned me down, I felt defenseless. It was pointless to ask him any more questions. Nor could I undo what had happened with Mateo and Luke.

Even though I had it in my head that Darnell didn't want anything more to do with me, I still needed to thank him for cooking chicken for me. I didn't want to make us both uncomfortable by doing it in person so an anonymous gift would be best. His community garden came to mind. Those kids had struggled to dig in the dirt with worn and rusted tools.

I opened my laptop and searched for Mt. Hope Community Garden. After a few links via the Billy Taylor Park Facebook page, I sent a message to the page organizer saying that I wanted to make an anonymous donation of $250 toward the community garden.

A few minutes later, I received a message from the Facebook page saying they would gladly accept my kind contribution and directed me to call a phone number with my information.

After I did my good deed, I felt better about myself and the kids it would help. I wandered into my kitchen and opened the fridge. Why did I bother when I didn't cook? There was not much of a selection: a couple of lonely eggs, some takeout leftovers, a bottle of white wine, and 12 pounds of cheese from my Uncle Charlie.

"Eh." I scrunched my nose at the limited offerings and shut the fridge door. My pantry wasn't any better. Maybe I shouldn't have given that crab cake to Mrs. Patterson.

I ambled back into the family room and pulled up Tinder on my phone. Even though I had no interest in a real relationship with someone else, perusing the cute pics of eligible men brought me some entertainment.

My fingers clicked on a shot of a man with sunglasses on and a baseball cap. Show me your face, dude. Nope.

Another smoking a cigarette. No thanks. I wanted to keep my healthy lungs. Swipe left.

A third with a pretty woman on his arm. His bio said he and his wife were looking for another woman to join them. Hard pass.

A few hot men popped up on my feed and I swiped right just for fun. It was up to them to contact me but I was not about to make the first move. If not, no harm, no foul.

I thought more about what my grandpa said about marriage. If Darnell would have me, I could see myself marrying him. He was an amazing guy and he could see through my nonsense. I needed someone who respected himself and me. Darnell was it. He made me laugh and think. He was one of the best people I knew. I was such a fool to let him go and now I was dealing with the aftermath. I thought about him all the time and my life was better because of him. Plus, it didn't hurt that he was hot. We could have made cute babies together. He would be an amazing dad.

I wanted Darnell. But he didn't want me.

CHAPTER 25

The next day at work, I headed to Jenna's desk at noon so that we could attend Mateo's gym opening.

"You ready?" I asked her.

"Yep," she said. "We can go in our work clothes, right?" Jenna motioned to her short black skirt and wedge sandals.

"Yes. Probably can't do a class dressed like that, but you could sign up for one later I'm sure."

We hopped down the stairs to the sidewalk and wove our way through foot traffic on Dorrance Street. A steady stream of cars raced by us, spitting exhaust into the city air. Horns honked and mufflers revved. As our heels clicked along the cement, we walked by Johnson

194

and Wales University buildings, several banks, mortgage brokers, and restaurants full of lunch-time diners. Downtown Providence understood our ups and downs of life, offering coffee shops to wake us up in the morning and pub libations in the evening to help us forget about bad days.

A few blocks later, we approached the four-story building that now boasted *Fit Club* banners where the lease signs used to be. The last time I was here, Mateo and I had our lunch-time quickie amongst dusty, framed-out fitness areas. That was over two weeks ago. Jenna and I entered the now-pristine venue where rows of treadmills, ellipticals, and free weight machines stretched out before us. A floor-to-ceiling mirror extended along an entire wall. Jump ropes and elastic bands hung from hooks on another wall. On nearby open shelves, free weights and kettlebells waited to be used. Inspirational messages encouraged gym rats to do *One More*.

A group of fitness gurus gathered in the far corner, circling Mateo. He acknowledged us with a smile and waved us over.

"Hey," he said to me dismissing his staff, "so glad you could make it." Mateo wore a black *Fit Club* tank top that exposed waves of drool-worthy tanned muscles. I smiled, remembering what those arms and the rest of his magnificent body could do to me.

"Everything looks great." I nodded toward the well-lit workout space. "Good for you."

"Thanks." Mateo's blue eyes drifted toward Jenna. "Who's your friend?"

"This is Jenna. That's right… you two never met."

"Pleasure to meet you." Jenna offered her hand and a smile to Mateo with her Southern charm. "I've heard lots about you."

"I hope it's all good." He smiled at her with stunning white teeth.

"Of course," I said.

"I like the pink in your hair." Mateo took an extra second studying Jenna, then gestured toward another corner of the room where a buffet was set up. "You ladies go help yourself to the spread. There's salad, black bean quesadillas, chicken tacos, and you know I had to offer up some baked plantains, sweet bread, and washboard cookies."

"Like your washboard abs?" I joked.

"Yeah."

I expected Mateo to banter more with me, but he couldn't keep his eyes off of Jenna.

"Thank you for inviting us," Jenna said, finally breaking Mateo's mesmerization.

"My pleasure," he said.

Jenna turned and headed toward the food and I was quick on her heels, leaving Mateo behind.

I grabbed her by the elbow once we were out of earshot of him. "Mateo was totally checking you out."

"He was not." She rolled her eyes at me.

"Oh, come on. He barely spoke to me once he saw you. Completely blew me off."

"He said he liked the pink strand in my hair." She curled it between her fingers. "That means he's gay because no straight man has ever taken notice of my hair."

"I can assure you he's not gay!" I hissed, letting go of her arm.

Jenna rolled her eyes at me again and grabbed a plate. She turned away and plucked a few things to eat from the lunch buffet. A few other guests formed a line behind us.

"Oh, come on! How can a straight man look that hot, like my pink hair, and *not* be gay?" Jenna volleyed. "The gay men in Charleston are all like that."

"For the last time, he's not gay." I snagged a plate from the front of the buffet and followed Jenna. "You know I went out with him."

I picked up some of the Portuguese food that Mateo had brought in for the special occasion and plunked some down on my plate.

"Okay, let's say he isn't gay and that my gaydar is all messed up because of that jerk who dumped me." Jenna stopped and gaped at me, her plate at an angle within inches of letting the food roll off. "You still went out with him. I don't want your sloppy seconds." She narrowed her eyes at me, the crease between her brows formed a deep V.

"If Mateo asks you out and you want to do it, I will gladly step aside."

"Thank you for the pity date. You don't think I can find someone myself?" she challenged.

"That's not what I meant." I took a step back, hoping to get out of the way of Jenna's unprecedented wrath.

She glared at me, waiting for an answer.

198

"I meant that Mateo clearly thinks you're cute and he has never stared at me the way he looked at you just now." I nodded toward the corner of the gym where we previously stood. Mateo was conversing with his staff again but glanced up at Jenna a few times with his piercing blue eyes. I was now his second choice.

"That's better. Keep going," Jenna spoke.

Under her sweet Southern roots, I think Jenna secretly loved taunting me. She had quickly acclimated to being a Yankee where we northerners didn't think twice about saying something snarky.

"I don't stand a chance anymore."

Jenna laughed at me. "I'm teasing you. I would never let a guy come between us and I know I can snag one even though I'm a little rusty. I'd go out with Mateo if he asked me. But it was fun watching you sweat a little. Ironic that we're in a gym."

"You got me. Okay, good." I half-hugged her, careful not to tip either of our plates. "Besides, who else besides me could tell you what Mateo likes in bed?"

Jenna and I enjoyed our lunch, signed up to be members at the gym, and then headed back to work.

Later that afternoon, my phone buzzed with a text from Mateo. Ur friend Jenna is a dime. Is

she single? Do u mind if I ask her out?
Jenna would be happy to learn this.

I chuckled at Mateo's text. It was near duplicate of the one Luke had sent me about Ebony the previous week.

Go ahead. Yes, she's single, I replied.

U sure ur ok with this?

I appreciated Mateo's concern. I had hot memories of us in bed together, but I never imagined a real future with him. He and I had insane physical chemistry, but that's all it was. I never felt like I could tell him my deepest secrets or share my vulnerabilities with him. I never found that level of comfort with him. He and Jenna would be good together. My hot nights with Mateo had come to an end.

Yes I'm sure, I wrote. We're cool.

* * * *

The next morning, Jenna jumped out of her seat when I walked in the door.

"You're not gonna believe my night last night!" she shrieked. Her pale skin glistened with a warm glow.

"Why? What happened?"

"Mateo is amazing," she gushed, briefly closing her eyes and holding her fists close to her chest as if she was hugging a soft blanket.

"Because he couldn't get enough of you? And you used an entire box of condoms?"

"No!" Jenna came down off of her high and scoffed at me. "We were up all night *talking*."

"Talking?" I raised an eyebrow at her. Mateo and I spent most of our nights together naked.

"He's so sweet. He texted me late yesterday afternoon and asked me out for dinner. He even brought flowers. We spent four hours at dinner because we clicked so well. Then after he paid, he said he didn't want to say goodnight to me. Me either. So, we found a 24-hour diner and spent the rest of the night there talking about anything and everything."

"Wow. That's great."

"Did you know he was born in a small town in Portugal and then his family moved here when he was two?"

"No, I didn't."

"And he has five older sisters and they taught him how to salsa?" Jenna shimmied in her seat as if she was dancing.

I never knew that Mateo had so many sisters nor that he was born in Portugal. The subjects never came up. Obviously, Jenna and Mateo were a better match than he and I.

"And he asked me all about growing up in Charleston, what I liked and didn't like about living here, and if I ever saw myself as a mom."

"Sounds like you had a great night." I grinned at Jenna. She deserved a good guy. "Are you seeing Mateo again?"

"Of course," Jenna spoke as if I had said something blasphemous. "We're going dancing tonight at his Portuguese Social Club. He's going to teach me how to salsa."

"I'm so happy for you." I skirted around her desk and hugged her. "I can't wait to hear all about it."

As I walked to my desk and tripped over the darn carpet, I pondered what had happened to me in the past few weeks. All three of the major men in my life showed up at my house at the same time. Then all three of them drifted out of my life. Two of them ended up with my friends and the third rejected me. I was happy for my friends. I really was. But my bed and my heart were empty. What had I done to upset the relationship gods?

202

I didn't want to start all over again on Tinder and weed out the wrong men. My chest tightened and my heartfelt void. I slumped into my chair and couldn't imagine where my life was going.

One thing was certain: I was never taking Ambien again!

CHAPTER 26

On Friday afternoon, I shut down my computer to go home. I didn't get a chance to check my personal email because I was too busy during the day with work stuff. I made a mental note to check it later. My phone rang with a call from my grandpa and I snatched it up.

"How's my favorite peanut buttah cup?" he sang into the phone.

"Happy this week is over. It was bad."

"Why? What happened?"

"Eh. I'll explain tomorrow at dinner."

"Sounds like a Johnnie Walkah Blue night again."

"But I'm not cooking."

"Thank goodness!" Grandpa laughed heartily. "Don't worry. I'll find something to make for us."

"Thanks, Grandpa. I'll see you then."

I hung up, grabbed my bag, and headed out the door. Jenna was already gone. She must have skipped out early to get ready to go dancing with Mateo.

Ten minutes later, I pulled up in front of my house and found Mrs. Patterson dusting the late Mr. Patterson's giant anchor in the front yard. Old people tended to do strange things. She had her back to me and didn't hear my car with her hit or miss hearing, so I easily grabbed my mail and snuck into my house. Most times I was fine chatting with her, but today was not one of those days.

Inside, I hit my speed dial and placed a delivery order with PieZoni. A couple of slices to be delivered in fifteen minutes. What could be better? Hopefully, this was a good sign that my weekend would be an improvement on the preceding days.

I grabbed a bottle of white wine from the fridge to pour myself a glass. Uncle Charlie's cheese still had not found a permanent home. I wasn't sure what to do with it, but I needed to figure it out soon before the cheese expired. I hated to waste it. The 100 tiny handcuffs from

Plenty of Fish in the Ocean State

Niki still sat in the box in the corner of my living room waiting to be used. Fortunately, they couldn't expire like the cheese, but I had no clue how I'd use them. Leave them out for my mouse tenant and hope that she and her furry friends might use them in a weird mouse orgy? Probably not.

While sipping on the wine, I sorted through my mail that had accumulated on the countertop throughout the week. Relentless credit card offers. A circular from an unclaimed freight furniture store. An envelope from AARP even though I was decades away from retiring. Coupons for a landscaper that I couldn't afford. All of it went in the trash.

A few minutes later, my doorbell rang. On my way to the front door, I snagged a few bills from my wallet.

"Hi! Here's your pizza." A young delivery man with a crooked baseball cap stood on my porch holding a small cardboard box when I opened the door.

"Thank you. Keep the change." I exchanged the pizza for the money and closed the door.

The aroma of baked dough and garlic filled my living room. Mmm. Not much was better than pizza from PieZoni. With the pizza box on my coffee table, I settled on the couch, held a gooey slice in my hand, and opened my laptop.

I perused my emails. Unsolicited messages from recruiters offering jobs in Texas. Delete. Notifications from friends on Facebook. I'll read them later. A frantic message about a missing cat from the neighborhood group. If I see it, I'll return it. A few rows down, a new email address caught my eye. The subject line said: `I apologize.`

From Crazy Cooper.

What the hell? My week just went from bad to worse.

Cooper and I dated for a few years when I attended Villanova. He was a senior starter on the basketball team and I was a sophomore. He didn't earn my moniker Crazy Cooper until the end of our three-year relationship when his true personality surfaced. Not sure if any of his other exes called him that but he garnered it from me. The breaking point of our relationship came when he was playing in the NBA and sent me a text saying that I needed to show him more care when he was under so much stress. Was he kidding? I was not his mother, his personal assistant, nor his babysitter. I didn't speak to him for ten days after that. On the eleventh day, he sent an onslaught of texts calling me fucking trash and accusing me of sleeping around. The next day, he sent a nasty email telling me what a horrible person I was and that I needed to apologize to him. Not one to back down from a fight, I told him that he was a mean and vicious person and he owed me an apology, not the other way around. He didn't respond. The end-of-the-relationship signs were there all along but I refused to acknowledge them because I was so caught up in the fact that a popular basketball player was into me. After that last clash, I finally had enough and blocked him on my Facebook, Instagram, email, and my cell number.

He was the reason I left Philadelphia and returned to Providence. I hadn't had any contact with him in three years. The time away from him had helped me heal and become stronger even though my anger about the relationship still lingered. But I also wondered what he wanted. Curiosity outweighed recovery.

My fingers jittering, I clicked on his email.

He wrote:

Hi Reese, you probably never expected to hear from me again. I've learned a lot over the past few years and

208

```
that I owe you an apology for what I said
to you. Here it is: I'm sorry. I heard
you moved back home. I'm in Providence
for the next couple of days and would
love to see you if you are free. Let me
know.

        Cooper
```

No freaking way! Who did he think he was?! I had zero interest in seeing him after the way he spoke to me. Even though it happened three years earlier, the scars remained. He was the reason I broke up with Darnell. I slammed my fist on the coffee table, knocking my laptop to the floor. The screen shattered on impact.

Great. Now I needed to buy a new laptop.

My temples throbbed with rage. The last time I had a headache like this, an Ambien hangover clouded my brain. Why all of a sudden did Crazy Cooper contact me? Did I send him a walrus-influenced message during my blackout? I quickly checked my Sent folder searching for any evidence from that fateful night. Nothing. I exhaled in relief. At least I hadn't reached out to him and this was all his doing. Hopefully, I didn't see any more fallout from my doped-up night.

I rummaged through my bag and found my phone. I called Ebony, willing her to pick up.

"Hey girl," she said.

I skipped the pleasantries. "Crazy Cooper emailed me," I blurted.

"What? You're joking?"

"Dead serious."

"What does that nut job want after all this time?"

I wished I had known Ebony when I ended things with Crazy Cooper. She would have made the horrible breakup more bearable. Since then, she lent me an open ear any time I wanted to vent.

I scoffed because I still couldn't believe it myself. "He finally apologized for what he said to me three years ago and now he's in town and wants to see me."

"You have to go."

"What? No way." Why on Earth did Ebony think that was a good idea? Hell would have to freeze over for me to see him again. She knew how much I now despised Crazy Cooper. I had moved on since dating him. Even if I was now alone.

"You have to go," Ebony repeated. "Because if you don't go, some time down the road, when you aren't

210

so pissed at him, you'll kick yourself that you had the chance to get your closure and you didn't take it."

I hated when she was right. "Fine," I groaned. We didn't call Ebony The Queen of Queens for nothing.

"Here's what you do. You tell him exactly where to meet you and what drink to buy you. The ball is in your court, so to speak. If he doesn't show up or effs up your drink choice, you can tell him to pound sand. Be the bigger person."

Ebony had listened to my stories about how Crazy Cooper was notorious for being late. He once made me miss my flight on my way back to Philly when I was visiting him in Orlando for a game because he couldn't get me to the airport in time. Another time, we were meeting friends of mine and he didn't start getting ready to go out until five minutes after we were supposed to be there. Forty-five minutes later, we showed up. I was so embarrassed but didn't want to fight in front of my patient friends.

Ebony spoke again, "Once you get your closure, then you can finally move on."

"Okay, I'll do it. But don't think I like it." I rolled my eyes even though Ebony couldn't see me.

"Atta girl. You got this."

211

I imagined her doing a fist pump.

"Thanks. I'm glad I talked to you. You always know what to say."

"Call me when you're done. I wanna hear what happens."

"You got it."

I hung up with Ebony and the pulsing in my temples had lessened. She had a way of talking me off a ledge. If I hadn't spoken to her, Crazy Cooper might have endured my worst wrath and found my knee in his groin.

Since my laptop was broken, I was left replying to Cooper via my phone. I made a mental note to get a new computer at some point over the weekend.

I wrote:

Hi Cooper- I found the near-impossible restraint not to write "Crazy Cooper." Good to hear from you. I sucked in my breath. Being nice to him was like forcing a dog to like a cat, but I had to push myself to do it. Sure, we can meet up while you're in town. I didn't want to sound overly happy to see him, but not bitter either. Even though I was. Meet me at Wickenden Pub at 7:00. Order

212

Plenty of Fish in the Ocean State

me a Jameson. **Grandpa would be proud.** See you then.

Crazy Cooper replied within five minutes: Great! Looking forward to it. A glass of Jameson will be waiting for you.

No one was around to bet that he wouldn't be there on time.

It was now 6:00. I had an hour to change out of my work clothes and drive over to the pub. I purposely didn't give Crazy Cooper the address, so it was up to him to find it. Not my fault if he got lost.

After changing into jeans and a casual t-shirt, I left my house at 6:40. The trip to Wickenden Pub was usually a 10-minute drive. Assuming there was no traffic, I would get there 10 minutes early and have plenty of time to wait for Crazy Cooper.

I kept reminding myself that I needed closure otherwise the wounds would never heal. Then I could have a real relationship with an adult. That was the driving force behind everything. I needed that to move on. I could forgive Crazy Cooper for what he said to me, but I would never forget.

CHAPTER 27

When I parked my Impala in the lot near Wickenden Pub at 6:50, I noticed a black convertible Jaguar with an out-of-state tag parked in front of the building. Nooo. That couldn't be Crazy Cooper's car, could it? No way was he here on time, let alone early.

I pushed through the oak doors to a nearly empty pub. The late crowd hadn't come yet. Music blared from overhead speakers as the bartender washed glasses. Libation experts filled a couple of the booths and a few people settled at the bar stools.

There he was. My eyes drifted over to other patrons' faces and then landed on Cooper.

Not only was he on time, but he was at the bar before me. Crazy Cooper unsuccessfully hunkered on a bar stool; his long legs bent under the counter. At six-foot-nine and a redhead, he was hard to miss even if he tried to squat down to be at the same height as the rest of us normal-sized, average-haired humans.

When he saw me, he immediately stood from the barstool and took a few steps toward me; his arms outreached as if he wanted to hug me.

"Hi, Reese. You look amazing."

My body tensed and a scowl formed on my face. I leaned away from him and held a hand up to block him. "Is it okay if we don't hug?"

"Sure." Crazy Cooper realized he wouldn't win me over with a cheap embrace and settled back on his stool. "How've you been? It's good to see you. You look great."

I glared at him, unsure of his ulterior motive. "Why are you here?" I blurted.

"I was in town and wanted to see you." He handed me an amber drink that had been sitting on the bar in front of him. "This is for you. Jameson, just like you ordered."

215

"Thank you." I hesitantly took a sip of the drink. I didn't trust it or him. Then I kept my distance.

So far Crazy Cooper had done everything I asked him to do in the past two hours, but it wasn't enough for me to give him any slack. I wasn't convinced he had changed. I should have dumped him after our first Christmas together and not wasted any more time with him. Back then, he didn't get me a Christmas present nor even acknowledged that I got him something. I had come home for winter break, sent his gift in the mail, and had to ask him if he received it. I was so hurt but ended up forgiving him. That should have been my first clue that he was a self-absorbed nutcase. It could have saved me a lot of heartache.

Once he was drafted in the NBA and while I was still at Villanova, he was able to pay for flights to bring me to his games once a month. The mini vacations were filled with lots of expensive meals, posh hotels, and spa treatments. The lavish long-distance relationship made it easy for me to avoid issues with him.

"I have to ask you," he said. "What happened between us?"

"You called me fucking trash!" I shrieked. I caught myself losing my temper and took a quick deep

216

breath to calm myself. I refused to let him see me angry after all these years. I was better than that.

Were the relationship gods testing me yet again?

"Yes," he sighed, raking a hand through his red hair. "I'm very sorry about that. I like to think I've matured since then."

Even though the charming words flowed out of his mouth, they were futile.

Cooper spoke again, "But what happened before that? What led to it?" He motioned to me. "By the way, you look amazing!"

Oh my god, he didn't know! He had no recollection of what he did to cause the emotional avalanche. And he offered pretty, empty words. Was he that dense and self-absorbed? My vote was yes.

"You--" I could barely get the words out without a crack in my voice. "You told me… that you… needed me to give you more care when you were under so much stress." I glowered at him with daggers for eyes. That in and of itself might not have been so bad, but I had reached my breaking point with him by that time. "I mean, who says that? What normal, mature adult would have the audacity to say that to the person they are

217

dating?" I carefully chose my words. "How could you honestly think that I wouldn't get upset about that?"

"You're right," Cooper whispered. "I was playing for a new team and took the pressure out on you. I'm sorry."

"I was hurt at first and then you blasted me with 50 texts telling ME what a horrible person I was!" I screeched. The bartender stopped washing his glasses and stared at me for a moment because I disrupted the din of the bar. So much for not losing my temper. "You're--" I couldn't bring myself to say *crazy*. I hoped I had matured since then too.

"An ass?" he finished my sentence.

"Yes. An ass." I scoffed and shook my head in disgust. "I should have paid more attention to the red flags. Ironic since you have red hair. You were insanely jealous of my male classmates, my male neighbors, my exes, and even my male professors. One time you called me six times when I was out with friends as if you were lifting your leg and marking your territory!" My fingers curled tightly around the glass of whiskey, tempting to break it.

"I'm sorry."

218

"I should have dumped you so many times," I gritted through my teeth. "When my parents had their 25th wedding anniversary party, you refused to come with me, because you didn't want to be around my family. What did they ever do to you? That's so insulting and hurtful." The more painful memories that I conjured up, the angrier I became.

"You're right," he said. "I should have come." He lowered his head in shame.

"Then, on our last vacation together, you left me high and dry for days because you needed to get your workout in. And you blamed me for forcing you to go. We had it planned for months!" I glared at him, hands on my hips, daring him to defy me.

Bottled-up anger pushed me to keep going and I raised a finger toward Crazy Cooper's face. "You constantly told me to 'tell you something sweet' as if you needed that continuous affirmation from me. Who *does* that?" I sneered.

I also wanted to say that he was the most selfish and needy person I had ever met, but I held my tongue. The basketball fans at Villanova made him out to be some kind of god and he relished the fame, acting like I should be lucky to be with him. He was now 32 years old but I would always remember him behaving like a three-year-old who demanded constant attention. That kind of relationship was no longer for me.

"I get it and I'm sorry," Cooper said.

I blew out a discontented sigh and swallowed my Jameson.

"Did you see my car out there?" he asked proudly.

"Which one?" I already knew the answer.

"The black convertible parked out front."

"Oh, that's yours?" I feigned interest. How someone as tall as he fit into a car like that was a question for another day.

"You wanna go for a ride in it?"

Under other circumstances, I would have loved to take a trip in a fast car like that, but I didn't want to be at the mercy of Crazy Cooper's advances with no way to escape. I was not about to leap out of a moving car if I didn't like what he said or did.

"I don't think so."

"You sure? It's a sweet ride." He grinned at me, probably remembering that his smile used to convince me to do other things.

"I'm sure."

"Maybe some other time."

I doubted I would change my mind.

"So, are you… are you... dating anyone?" He chewed his lip as if he was unsure if he wanted to know the answer.

My mind was filled with thoughts about Luke and Mateo. And Darnell. All of them had recently drifted out of my life, directly and indirectly by my influence.

"No."

Cooper spoke, "Is there any chance you would want to try again with me? I've missed you and I promise I will be better. You are the best thing that ever happened to me."

He stood from his stool, towering over me. I glanced to my side hoping that no one in the bar took notice of the professional basketball player among them. I didn't need that kind of attention right now.

The anger inside me subsided momentarily. I swallowed hard and studied him, trying to figure out his angle. He *seemed* remorseful and he didn't once blame me for his previous horrendous behavior, like he had many times before. Now three years later, I was still angry at him. My life had changed for the better but being with Cooper again would drag me back down. His

221

previous actions had fueled a rampant inferno deep inside me. The embers had set ablaze years ago, but he now tempted them with a match to ignite again. I didn't want to be that person. Even though he claimed he was better, I didn't believe him. I didn't want to take care of a needy toddler trapped inside a man's body. In my eyes, he would never change. But I had.

"I'm sure you've had plenty of girls falling all over you since then," I sneered. Maybe he got bored with the other chicks and thought I would still be waiting for him?

"Well…"

I quickly held a hand up to stop him. "You know what, I don't want to know."

"But none of them compared to you," Cooper said. "You are perfect for me."

"No. I can't. I'm sorry."

"It's okay. It's cool." He sat back down on the stool, more at my level. "I have to confess. I came here because a head coaching job opened up at Providence College and I'd leave playing pro and take it if I had a chance to be with you."

For the first time, I was taken aback by his maturity and desire to change to be with me. Maybe he had transformed into a better person, but I wasn't

222

convinced. His past indiscretions still angered me. I refused to let them consume me. Most guys didn't take a risk like this to dig up an old flame, but I didn't care. He had hurt me too much.

"I don't think so."

His shoulders fell and a slight frown formed on his face, but I couldn't let myself go backward. I had come too far, even if I wasn't dating anyone.

A few people entered the pub, interrupting us. I wondered how long we had been there. Cooper had said a lot, but what else was left to discuss? We had no future, nor did I want to be friends with him. No need to delay the inevitable.

"Look, I gotta go." Even though I had no specific place to go except home, I didn't want to stay there with him.

"Are you sure?" He reached for my hands but realized what he had done and retreated.

"I'm sure." I downed the rest of my drink. "Thanks for the whiskey."

"My pleasure." He smiled at me. "If I'm in town again, maybe we can get together again?"

"Maybe." I wanted to say no, but my kindness won out. I was trying to be a better person.

I left Cooper in the bar, letting the past slam shut when I walked out the door. Ebony was right. I finally got my closure. The Queen of Queens reigned again.

Once in my car, I picked up my phone to tell her the good news. I scoped the area outside the window to make sure Crazy Cooper hadn't followed me.

"Crazy Cooper is out of my life." I did a fist pump even though Ebony couldn't see me.

"Atta girl!"

CHAPTER 28

The next day, after I bought myself a new laptop, I settled into a chair at my grandpa's kitchen table. Three fingers of Johnnie Walker Blue pooled in a glass in front of me.

Grandpa hunkered into the chair next to me and clinked his glass against mine. He pushed his specs up his nose. "Now that we have our drinks, tell me about your week."

He had made a pot of his famous chowder for us and it was simmering on the stove.

"It went from bad to worse," I groaned.

"Why? What happened?"

"Do you remember Cra--? I mean Cooper." I took a swig of my whiskey.

"The one you dated who played basketball at Villanova and went pro?"

"Yeah, him. I never told you the whole story about why things went south with him. I'll get to that, but he showed up here yesterday and asked me if I wanted to get back together."

"What did you say?"

"I wanted to tell him to go pound sand, but I was nice and politely declined." If Ebony hadn't prepped me to be civil, she might have had to bail me out of jail.

Grandpa chuckled and swallowed some of his whiskey.

"That doesn't sound so bad." Grandpa leaned back in his chair; his right arm stretched out over the top.

"That's because I never told you the details of why I dumped him. It's why I call him Crazy Cooper."

Grandpa laughed out loud and finished his whiskey. "I have all night."

I continued, "He's nuts. Or at least he was. He claims he isn't now, but I don't believe him. There's so

226

much I never told you while we were dating. It's a long story. Let me see if I can sum it up."

"Looks like I'll need more for this story." He poured himself another three fingers of liquor.

"I fell for Cooper pretty early on and was infatuated with the fact that someone as popular as him could be into me. Call it college insecurity."

"You've come a long way." Grandpa raised his glass in a toast toward me.

"Thanks." I clinked my glass with his. "Things were good in the beginning. He treated me well and seemed genuinely interested in what I did. But it must've been a sham because as soon as he felt I was his, he gaslighted me. Do you know what that is?"

"Of course. I'm not 90."

I laughed at Grandpa's self-deprecation.

"Cooper was needy and insanely jealous. He'd growl at me like a dog if I ever mentioned any other guy. Even if it was the mailman! For some dumb reason, I put up with it and hoped it would get better."

"It didn't." Grandpa offered me a supportive smile.

"Right. And he was terrible with money. He blew it on stupid stuff like taking his laundry to a wash and

227

fold instead of investing in a washer and dryer. And he never paid his bills on time. I knew of at least six times that the electric company turned off his lights because he didn't pay them. Then he blamed them for shutting off his electricity. He had the money but didn't make the effort to pay his bills. He was like that with me too. Blamed me for not reminding him to do it." Now that I said it, I wondered if he was making car payments or if the Jaguar would be repossessed soon. Not my problem anymore.

"*Why* were you with him in the first place?" Grandpa arched a white eyebrow at me.

"He was good to me most of the time. And I was blinded by the extravagant lifestyle that he could give me. My friends in college were so jealous." I stared off into the depths of the kitchen. Evil thoughts of borrowing Paul Revere's knife to slash Cooper's tire entered my head. But I quickly brushed them away. "It was exhausting being with him. He constantly complained about everything and thought he was so much better than everyone else. He treated me like I should be lucky to have him."

"He was lucky to have *you*." Grandpa gestured toward me with his glass.

228

"Yeah, because I put up with his nonsense for years. I still can't believe I wasted my time like that."

"Don't be so hard on yahself. You were young and naive."

I laughed out loud. "Yeah, that must be it. A year after Cooper made pro, I honestly expected him to propose. He even hinted toward it. You don't know this, but I told him to give me a reason to stay with him because I was getting impatient. He flew me out to L.A. when he was playing the Lakers, took me out to this fancy restaurant along the beach, had a bottle of champagne in front of us, and then he presented me with a promise ring. A freaking promise ring! What a joke. He totally wasted my time." I scoffed in disgust.

"You still haven't gotten to the paht where you broke up with him." Grandpa smirked at me.

"Oh, right." I gulped down some whiskey in preparation to tell the rest of my tale. "Very long story short, he flipped out on me because I wasn't catering to his neediness and called me fucking trash."

"I'll kill him." In an unexpected action for an old man, Grandpa leaped from his chair and reached for Paul Revere's knife above the sink. I didn't need to slash Cooper's tires. Grandpa had other plans.

"It's okay. It's okay. It's all good. I took care of it."
I raised my hand and made lowering motions in the air,
trying to calm Grandpa down. He stopped inches from
the knife and faced me.

"You sure?" Grandpa's face hardened,
something I had rarely seen. "I'm an old man. I don't
mind spending the rest of my days in jail."

I wasn't sure whether to laugh or cower at his
intent. He relented and sat back down in the chair next
to me.

"Yes, I'm sure." I held his wrinkled hand in mind.
"But I appreciate you defending my honor."

"You're my favorite peanut buttah cup."

"Thanks, Grandpa." I smiled wide at my number
one fan. "Cooper might be able to have all these
hookups while he's on the road, but he'll never have a
real relationship if he keeps treating women like that."

"You've moved onto biggah and bettah things."

"I have." I gave my grandpa a bright, courageous
smile.

Grandpa stood again and stirred his bubbling
chowder at the stove. "Speaking of that, how are things
with Dahnell?"

"I think that's over," I sighed.

"Why?" Grandpa stopped stirring the soup and gaped at me. The scent of salty clams filled the air. No wonder the ladies loved his chowder.

"He didn't want me." I raked a hand through my blonde hair. "I screwed up. You heard about what happened at the dance. Then I saw him on Wednesday at his food truck and it started off well when he kissed me on the cheek but then it quickly went downhill."

Grandpa stared at me expectantly.

I continued, "Darnell asked me about Luke and Mateo. I couldn't give him a straight answer and he walked off. And that was the end of it." I shook my head and blew out a low sigh.

"Do you love him?" Grandpa took a step toward me and put his hand on my shoulder.

"Yeah. I do." I cupped my chin in my hand and gazed away. "He's the best man I've ever met. He gives me happiness that I didn't know I could feel. I want him and only him." I suddenly had no qualms about sharing my feelings about Darnell. Even with my octogenarian grandpa.

"What if you had a second chance with him? What would you say?"

231

I appreciated that Grandpa asked the hard questions.

"I'd say that I messed up and would do anything to be with him again. It was always him. The one who got away. The love of my life." I shrugged weakly, knowing that my pipedream would never come to fruition.

"You'll be okay, Resee. I know it." Grandpa went back to his chowder and ladled the creamy concoction into some bowls for us. "In the meantime, here's why all the ladies love my chowdah."

CHAPTER 29

On Monday morning, I woke up at 5:00 with a jolt. The events from the past week had weighed on me and clouded my head. I still had a few hours before I needed to get to work, but sleep was not in my favor. I pulled myself out of bed and dragged myself to the open window.

Outside, inky bands filled the sky. The sun wouldn't be up for another hour, but birds sang cacophonous chords in nearby trees, pulling dreamers from their slumber. I drew in a deep breath, inhaling scents of the early morning. Mrs. Patterson's flower bed sent sweet aromas of begonias and zinnias upward. Even though it was a mile away, the residual funk from

Providence River made its way to my sleeping neighborhood.

I needed to clear my head and a run would do me good. In college, I often ran eight to ten miles at a time with Crazy Cooper. But these days, I had no desire or time to go that far, despite Ebony's constant invitation to join her. After I pulled on a sports bra and running shorts, I laced up my sneakers, piled my hair into a topknot, and hopped down the steps. In the kitchen, I downed a glass of water and headed out the door.

Mrs. Patterson's house was quiet, as were most of the homes on our street. At her corner, I ran west along Mauran Avenue, with nothing but the impending sunrise accompanying me. My soles thumped along the asphalt, tapping in rhythm with my breathing. For the first half-mile, there were no sidewalks, so I ran down the middle of the deserted street. Sweat soaked my clothes and hair.

With the streetlights illuminating my path, I crested the hill and then coasted down the road toward the river. A few tugboats chugged along the water, on their way to be unloaded at the docks. I turned left at the end of Mauran Avenue onto Water Street. With the river and marina on my right, I ran past a lot of dry-docked boats on my left. The salty ocean air filled my nose.

I left the main road and joined a jogging path along the river. More boats sailed by, filled with early morning hauls of quahog clams and fresh fish. I ran by the yacht club, knowing that the edge of the river was just over a mile from my house. I stopped to take a break near a small dock in Bold Point Park. A pickup truck was parked across the street.

In the shadows of orange and pink sunrise, I made out a silhouette of a man and a woman standing next to several large coolers on the narrow dock. Their backs were to me. I found it strange that they were waiting there when nothing else was happening around us. My heavy breathing must have given me away, as the man turned to face me.

"Reese?" he called to me. "Is that you?" He cupped a hand to his face as if it would help him see clearer in the early hours of the morning. He strode toward me, leaving his companion behind.

Darnell.

I puffed out a disgruntled sigh. Of all the times he ran into me and I was a sweaty mess. I patted down a few soaked hairs, hoping to look presentable.

"What are you doing here?" I said.

"Waiting for my haul for the food truck. I come here in the mornings to get fresh fish and quahogs."

When Darnell reached me, he gave me a quick hug and kissed my cheek. I cringed knowing that he didn't want to taste my sweat. I found it odd that he embraced me again, remembering the last time we talked. I wasn't complaining, especially in front of his guest, but his contrasting personalities confused me.

"But this isn't the main dock?" I gestured toward the small, empty pier.

"No," Darnell said. "When I first contacted the skipper, he told me to meet him here in the mornings because it's easier for him to unload. I'll put everything in the coolers and take it in the pickup back to the food truck." He pointed to the vehicle across the street.

Darnell's friend left the pier and walked toward us. She appeared around our age, with her hair pulled back into two braids, and had a bandana wrapped around her dark locks. She wore a paper-thin t-shirt that broadcasted the fact that she wasn't wearing a bra. I secretly admired her brazen attitude because I could never pull off something like that with my ample chest.

"He's almost here, babe," the young woman called. "He just called me."

Darnell turned to her. "Okay, thanks. Be right there."

Babe?

Who the hell was this woman and why was she calling Darnell *babe*? My mouth dropped open a little and a slight growl mumbled in my throat. I couldn't let Darnell pick up on the fact that I was shocked that he was with someone else. He had never mentioned it. He didn't owe me any explanation about her. I selfishly assumed that he was single since he had casually flirted with me many times over the past few weeks. Seconds ago, he kissed me on the cheek. The realization finally hit me. He was merely being kind to me all this time and he had zero romantic feelings for me. All of the angst going through my head for the past week was for naught. I was so stupid.

Darnell faced me again.

"If you stick around, you can see the fresh clams and butterfish we pull right off the boat." Darnell scratched his beard. "We have some Maine lobster coming in, too."

"Ehh. I think I'll pass. I might lose my appetite for breakfast," I lied. In reality, I wasn't interested in spending the morning with Darnell and his girlfriend. I crossed my arms against my chest.

"Well, you can always come by the food truck and get it cooked there." Darnell grinned at me.

The late summer sun splashed beams of yellow and orange into the sky.

"I should get going." I wiped the back of my hand along my soaked forehead. Running wasn't the only thing that made me break a sweat. "I still have to run home and then get ready for work."

"It was good to see you, Reese." Darnell reached for me and kissed me on the cheek again.

For someone who was dating someone else, he was tempting her jealousy. If it was me, I would never kiss someone else in front of my boyfriend.

"You too."

I left Darnell and his girlfriend at the dock and ran home with a vengeance. The whole time I wanted to kick myself for being such a fool. At home, I stormed up the squeaky stairs to the second floor. When I turned the knob to my bedroom door, the old bronze handle fell off the shank into my hand. "Stupid old houses!" I shrieked to no one and threw it on the floor to fix another day.

I stomped my way into the shower, throwing my clothes off in the wake of the devastation. Bits of wall plaster fluttered down to the floor behind me.

In the shower, I rubbed my skin raw. I couldn't believe I let myself fall for Darnell again. He was only being kind the entire time. Because that's how he was with everyone. I wasn't special in his eyes.

I dressed for work, putting on grey trousers and a plain white blouse. The drab clothing would help me keep a low profile because I was in no mood to be outgoing today. I barely did my hair and makeup.

Even though I told Darnell I was planning on eating breakfast, I had no appetite. I could get coffee at work if I felt better. Seeing him with his girlfriend burned into my memory bank. I still couldn't believe it. I rubbed absently at my arms.

In a mental fog, I drove to work, mindlessly weaving the Impala in and out of traffic. If any other commuters were pissed off by my aggressive driving, I didn't care. My car was made of steel and if we got into a collision, I would win.

As I parked my car, my phone rang with a call from Val.

"Yeah?" I groaned as I started the two-block trek through downtown to my office building.

"Good morning to you, too."

"Sorry. I've had a rough morning."

"It's only 8:00. What happened?"

"I ran into Darnell. Literally. And his girlfriend."

"Oh." I imagined Val offering me a sympathetic frown.

"I don't get it though." I stopped in my tracks on the sidewalk, trying to process everything that happened a couple of hours earlier. "He kissed me on the cheek in front of her. Twice."

"That doesn't make sense. I don't know what to tell you."

"Me either," I sighed. "He's not the kind of guy to play games. I know it."

"There are so many players out there and he's not one of them."

"He's a good guy. But not interested in me."

"You'll be okay. I know you will. You still coming out for Aidan's birthday on Saturday? We're going to the pub at seven. It'll be fun. I don't want you sitting in your house all weekend."

Val knew me too well. When my high school boyfriend broke up with me a week before Prom, Val insisted that I still go. I wanted to curl up with a gallon of Ben and Jerry's but Val dragged me to get my nails done and we got ready at my parents' house, preventing me from ditching her.

"I'll be there. Because I know if I don't come, you'll drag my butt there."

"You bet I will."

I laughed out loud, thankful for a friend like Val.

CHAPTER 30

On Thursday after work, I called my grandpa as I curled up on my lumpy couch. The past few days had been better for me. I didn't think about Darnell as much. Even though I still adored him, I was on my way to accepting the fact that we would not be together again. I got up every morning and no longer fantasized about snuggling with Darnell on our couch watching old movies or helping him cook up something wonderful in our kitchen. I resolved to eating dinner alone. Except for meals with my grandpa.

"Hi, Grandpa. Can we move our dinner on Saturday to Sunday?"

"Yeah, sure, Reese. Do you have a date?"

242

"No, a bunch of us are going out for Aidan's birthday."

"Sounds fun. Maybe I'll call one of the ladies from the community center and see if they want to go out for a night on the town."

"That's a great idea. Dorothy was totally crushing on you."

"And Chandra." Grandpa barked a hearty laugh.

"You're quite the player, Grandpa." I giggled. Who would have thought my grandpa would have a better love life than me? I should have offered to take him to Aidan's party. We'd have a great time.

"What can I say? The ladies love my chowdah."

I had to wonder if he used that word as a clean substitute for sex. I didn't want to know the answer.

After I hung up, I noticed a new text.

From Darnell.

He wrote: Good to see you the other morning. Hit me up :)

I didn't know what to think. Why would he send me a text like that when he had no interest in me? And what if his girlfriend found out? What would she think? As much as I cared for him, I didn't want to be the side chick. I didn't know anything about her, but she

243

deserved better than that. When did Darnell become that kind of guy?

I deleted the text without responding.

I wandered into my kitchen, opened the fridge, and the big block of cheese stared back at me. What was I going to do with it? I plucked a small piece off and popped it in my mouth. That gave me an idea. I tore another piece off, put it on a small plate for my furry roommate, and placed it on the floor in the corner of the kitchen. She would never eat 12 pounds of cheese, but I was sure she'd appreciate a snack.

After slipping on my Birkenstocks, I trudged outside to my garden. I had been neglecting it and vagrant weeds had encroached on the tomatoes and peppers. Red spheres begged to be picked. Some of the peppers had rotten spots on them. I plucked the ripest ones and tucked them into a makeshift bowl made with the lower half of my shirt. Within minutes, my top was sagging from the weight. I needed to bring my fresh loot inside and grab a bag for the rest.

As I turned to go into my house, Mrs. Patterson waddled up to me. Her grey eyes were full of hope.

"Good evening, deeyah." She held a bunch of freshly picked flowers in her wrinkled arms. Tonight, she wore green polyester pants, a paisley blouse, and a cardigan to ward off the cool dusk breeze. An aroma of Ben-Gay encircled her. "Would you like some?"

"Sure. Wanna trade?" I pointed to the vegetables against my stomach.

"Thank you, deeyah. I wish my sistah lived nearby. She loves tomatoes." Her dentures seemed loose in her mouth.

I exchanged a few tomatoes and peppers from my stash for her flowers.

"Well if she ever comes to visit you, I'll be happy to give her some." I was glad to unload my bounty since I wasn't cooking them. If trading goods with an old lady was what my evenings were going to be like from now on, then I'd make the best of them.

"That's nice of you." She cocked her head at me. "So how is that cute Porta-geese? I haven't seen him around here in a while."

"And you probably won't again," I sighed.

"Why's that, deeyah?" She gazed down as if I kicked her puppy.

"Because he's now dating my friend Jenna," I replied. "I introduced them."

"What?--"

I imagined the mouse fell off the wheel inside her head. She probably couldn't grasp that it was now okay for girls to offer up the men they dated to their friends. No more jealous competition like in her time. Or was it now honor among thieves?

"It's okay, Mrs. Patterson. I'm fine with it. They're better together." She didn't need to know that Mateo and I only had physical chemistry in common. The lust was fun. I'm not saying it wasn't. But where did it lead? I now had zero interest in acting like a sailor on shore leave. Darnell called me out on that kind of behavior and it blew up in my face. I wanted something that Jenna and Mateo now had. And Luke and Ebony for that matter. I was far from a prude, but I didn't want to waste my life anymore with shallow, meaningless sex.

CHAPTER 31

On Saturday night, I dressed in a draped tank top, snug jeans, and stack-heeled sandals. Even though I was solo at the party, I still wanted to look amazing. To my good fortune, I found street parking a block up from Wickenden Pub. Val's '72 Fiat was right in front, causing passersby to drool at the cool vintage car. I was certain not too many people cared about my old, weathered Impala. I decided against regifting the Danny DeVito cardboard cutout for Aidan. It would have to find another home some other day. Instead, I held a small wrapped box in my hands.

I entered the dark pub and found Val and Aidan in the back-corner booth. Pints of beer rested on the table in front of them. I hugged them, wished Aidan happy birthday, and took a seat across from Val. Her bald husband sat next to her. Even though Aidan was our age, he started losing his hair in his early 20s and decided to shave it all off.

"Ebony and Jenna just texted me and they're on the way," Val said. "With their dates."

"Luke and Mateo?" I asked.

"Yes. You okay with that?" Val studied me as if she was waiting for me to explode.

"We all swap clothes and shoes, why not swap guys," I laughed. "I'll be the seventh wheel. It'll be fun."

I nodded toward Aidan. "Aren't your friends coming too?"

"They'll be here later."

"Maybe you won't be the seventh wheel after all," Val smirked.

The bartender approached our booth, interrupting us. "What can I get for you?" he said to me.

I glanced over at the dozen taps attached to the top of the bar. "I'll take a Blue Moon."

"You got it." He left us.

"This is for you," I said to Aidan and pushed the gift in front of him. "Happy Birthday."

248

He unwrapped the paper and opened the box to find the 100 tiny handcuffs that my college roommate Niki sent for my birthday three weeks earlier.

Aidan held a few up for Val to see and cocked his head at me. "Ummm…"

"I thought you two could use some spice in the bedroom," I teased.

"Yeah, but they barely fit our pinkies!" Val joked.

"We can put them somewhere else too." Aidan winked at us.

Just then, Ebony and Luke approached the booth, his palm at the small of her back near the tips of her long braids.

"Happy Birthday Aidan," Ebony said as she reached to hug him. She settled in the booth next to me.

Luke extended a hand to Aidan then sat down in the booth next to Ebony.

The bartender returned with my beer and took Ebony's and Luke's orders.

"Put the next round on my bill," Ebony told the bartender. Then she turned to Aidan. "My birthday gift to you."

"She's cool like that." Luke grinned lovingly at Ebony and held her closer to him. "One of the smahtest women I've ever met."

I was happy that they were together. Looking at them, I never would have guessed they'd be a couple, but they seemed to be perfect for each other. I wanted that happiness too.

"How did you get Luke here on time?" I asked Ebony. "I didn't expect you two for another half hour."

"He's a reformed flake," she laughed and planted a kiss on his mouth.

"She's worth being on time for," Luke replied.

Ouch.

"Aww," Val cooed. "You are too cute."

"He's searching for his own place and I'm helping him pick out furniture," Ebony added.

"Do you respond to her texts right away now too?" I teased Luke.

Before he could reply, Jenna and Mateo sauntered up to our booth, hand in hand. Jenna slid in next to Val and across from me. Mateo pulled a chair from a nearby vacant table and joined us. The seven of us were the largest group in the dive bar.

"Happy Birthday Aidan," Jenna chimed.

250

He wrote: `Hi Reese. What's up?`

I furrowed my nose and both Jenna and Ebony noticed.

"What's wrong?" Ebony spoke for both of them.

"It's Darnell," I said. I tipped my phone toward them and showed them his text.

"This is good, right?" Jenna asked.

"No, not when he has a girlfriend," I sighed. "He was with her at the docks the other morning. She called him *babe*."

"Oh." Jenna slumped back in defeat.

"I don't get him," Ebony spoke. "He *seems* like a great guy. He's not a jerk at all and he genuinely cares about people. Why would he play games like this?"

"No idea." I shrugged.

"What're you goin' to do?" Jenna asked.

"Nothing," I said, and deleted the message.

The bartender came by a few minutes later with our pizza from Fellini's and a stack of paper plates. Val divvied up slices and handed them out. Once everyone had food and drinks in front of them, Val spoke. "Thanks, guys, for coming out for my hubby's birthday tonight!"

"Yes," Aidan added. "I appreciate it. Here's to a fun night." He raised his glass of beer and we all toasted him.

A half-hour later, Aidan's buddies showed up, bringing laughter and fun in their wake. When they approached our table, Aidan introduced them. "Everyone, this is Tyler, Julian, and Asher. Guys, this is everyone." His friends stood at our table and said hello to all of us.

Val leaned across the table and whispered to me, "Julian's cute. Aidan told me he's single and he's our age."

"Yeah, he is." I glanced over at Julian. He caught my eye and gave me a quick head nod. Julian was tall and lean; his hair buzzed into a fade. His smooth baby-faced cheeks made him appear younger than 30.

"Go say hi," Val urged me.

"Ehh," I moaned and shrugged my shoulders. Julian was cute, but I didn't feel like making the first move.

"Oh, don't be such a wuss," Val chided. "He's a nice guy. I've met him a few times."

"Fine, I'll do it for you because I know you'll give me a hard time about it." I edged my way out of the crowded table and stood.

Julian took a step closer to me and offered his hand. "Hi, I'm Julian."

"I heard," I said. I liked his confidence so far.

"How do you know Aidan and Val?" he asked. "They're good people."

"Yeah, I know. I've been best friends with Val since kindergarten." I glimpsed in her direction and she gave me a thumbs up. "You?"

"Aidan and I work together,' Julian answered. "About four years now." He motioned to my empty hands. "Can I get you a drink?"

"Yeah, that'd be great," I said. "I'm drinking Blue Moon."

"Good choice. Be right back. Don't go anywhere." Julian grinned at me and headed toward the bar. As he walked away, I studied him. Seemed nice. Super cute. Good manners. Since he worked with Aidan, he had a steady job. Hadn't made a rude comment. So far, so good. I glanced over at Val and the rest of our friends deep in conversation. She caught my eye and mouthed the words, "go for it."

Julian returned a few minutes later with two beers and handed one to me. "Here's to a good night with a beautiful woman." He raised his drink in a toast and I clinked my glass against his.

"Thank you."

Julian and I talked for the next half hour about being single in Providence. We compared war stories and laughed at our misfortunes. I had high hopes for him. If he asked me out, I would say yes. He could be a good way to get over Darnell.

In the middle of our conversation, Julian's phone rang with the ring tone "Just the Two of Us" by Grover Washington, Jr. He had good taste in music too. Another plus.

"Hi, Momma," he said into the phone. He raised a finger to me and mouthed that he'd be a minute.

"Yes, Momma, I'll be there tomorrow... Yes, ma'am..." I heard him say. "And next weekend too. Don't worry, Momma..."

Oh, no. Julian was a momma's boy. She had his weekends locked down. Did that leave any room in his life for anyone else? No wonder he had good manners. She taught him well. But thoughts of his momma coming over to his house unannounced flashed through my head. What if we planned a date and she called at the last minute and he bailed on me? What if he had to run every decision by her? I couldn't deal with that. Was this why he was single?

"I gotta go, Momma," Julian said. "I love you." He hung up and gave me his full attention. "Sorry about that. I hadn't talked to her in a while."

"When was the last time you spoke to her?" I wanted to give Julian the benefit of the doubt. After all, he was cute and sweet.

"When she told me what to wear to come here," he replied matter of factly.

Shoot me now.

CHAPTER 32

The next day, I sniffed the flowers that Mrs. Patterson had given me. I had put them in a vase on my kitchen table and the aromatic fragrances filled the room. It was a good start to lift my spirits. Especially after the bomb of meeting Julian the night before.

The flowers inspired me. If they could withstand the bipolar late-summer weather of Rhode Island and produce brilliant blooms, then so could I. I might not have a man in my life, but that didn't mean I couldn't succeed at something else. I needed to overcome my nemesis: cooking. After all, if I was to entice any serious relationship, it'd help if I could at least put something edible on the table.

My phone buzzed with a text from my dad.

`Saw this and thought of you. Love you!` He included a YouTube clip of a grill catching fire. Very funny. Thanks, Dad. I love you too.

How hard could it be to cook?

I take that back. It was plenty hard for me. But if I wanted to create something appetizing, I needed to battle my culinary demons. I grabbed my new laptop from the living room, set it on the kitchen counter, and searched for easy-to-make meals. My grandpa would be so proud--and surprised--if I brought dinner to him later. The first article to pop up was "25 Dinners You Won't Be Able to Mess Up." Surely, the author had never met me, so how could they be so confident? I might be the first one to mess up. With newly found determination and a tiny ounce of fear, I perused the first item: Baked Mushroom Risotto. The subtext said that risotto was one of the hardest dishes to cook perfectly and involved a lot of labor. That didn't bring a vote of confidence from me. Pass. The next few recipes were Spinach Lasagna Rollups, Crunchy Black Bean Tacos, and Roast Chicken with Brussel Sprouts. All of which sounded way too complicated. I thought the writer wanted these to be simple?

259

Then, at the bottom, I saw the winner: One Pot Wonder Chicken Lo Mein claiming three easy steps. That could work. I had the one pot, thanks to my mom.

Nervous, I read the recipe and then scanned it again so that I wouldn't miss any steps. The author must've read my mind when she said to swap a box of pasta noodles for real lo mein noodles. Knowing I had a box of linguine in the back of my pantry as a gift from my grandpa for a rainy day, I was off to a good start. My confidence was high.

Thanks to a recent trip to Stop & Shop, I added pre-cooked chicken tenders, baby carrots, and bell pepper. I didn't have the mentioned green onions, so I hoped that their absence wasn't a big deal. Then I added the pasta. The recipe called for soy sauce, garlic powder, corn starch, sugar, and red pepper flakes. Oh no! Aside from the sugar, I had no idea if I had any of those spices in my cabinet. In a panic, I swatted through boxes and plastic containers on the lower shelf and only came up with salt and pepper. And the extra bag of spices that Darnell had left behind when he cooked for me two weeks earlier.

I opened it up and inhaled the savory aroma. Mmm. I couldn't remember what was in the colorful

260

concoction, but Darnell had called it the flavor of the gods. Saying a quick prayer to those culinary gods begging for their approval, I dumped the mixture into the pot. Someone would win this cooking battle. If I didn't, I would die trying.

The final item on the recipe was chicken broth. My epicurean confidence dropped like a lead balloon. I didn't have any broth and I was afraid to leave a half-prepared recipe to get some at the store.

Google to the rescue.

On my laptop, I searched for substitutes for chicken broth. White wine! Who knew that one of my favorite drinks would be a suitable replacement? I opened the fridge and found a new bottle in the back. The recipe called for four cups of broth and, remembering my high school physics, I poured the one-liter bottle into the pot.

Now that everything was in the pot, I put the lid on it as per the recipe. That was easy. Next, it said to bring it to a rolling boil. What was a rolling boil? I didn't know there were different kinds of boils. Inhaling a deep breath, I turned the heat on high and hoped for the best.

Once the mixture rose and tapped the lid, I figured something was up. I didn't want another episode of soup splattered on the ceiling. The recipe instructed me to stir and reduce the heat to medium-low. I could handle that. Fortunately for me, my stove knobs had easy-to-read labels that said Medium-Low.

The recipe's author was right. I didn't mess it up. I won!

After the food cooked for fifteen minutes, Darnell's spice blend filled my kitchen with tangy aromas. Too bad I couldn't share my accomplishment with him. He would be so proud of me.

But I knew someone else I could share it with.

I picked up my phone and called my grandpa.

"How's my peanut buttah cup?" he asked.

"Good." I smiled through the phone. "I have a surprise for you."

"Is it a lifetime supply of Jameson?"

I laughed at his unbridled optimism to live another 25 years. "No, but it has to do with dinner tonight."

"Darnell cooked for us again?" he asked. "Even though you're not with him, that guy makes a wicked chicken."

"I wish that were true, but no. I think you'll still be surprised."

"I can't wait. See you tonight. 6:00?"

"I'll be there."

After I hung up the phone, I stirred my accomplishment. I had no plans to tackle a lasagna anytime soon, but who knew I could make a simple meal. There was hope for me yet.

* * * *

At 5:45, I held the covered pot of chicken lo mein in my arm the same way a running back carried a football. With my free hand, I picked up my phone from the table. At that moment, a text from Darnell appeared on the screen.

He wrote: `Hi Reese. Hope you're ok. Hit me up.`

With a nimble thumb, I deleted the message. That was the third text from Darnell since I encountered him at the docks with his girlfriend. As much as I still liked him, I refused to allow myself to get mixed up with another woman's man. I had my standards.

As I headed out the door, I grabbed my mail from the mailbox. The title of a new magazine caught my eye - *Cranes Today.* It was probably Mrs. Patterson's and delivered to me by mistake. I'd get it to her the next time I saw her.

Ten minutes later, Grandpa met me at his front door.

"What's in the pot? A coupla live lobstahs?" He took it from my arms and I stepped into the foyer next to him.

"No, our dinner."

"Our dinner?"

"Yeah." I puffed out my chest. "I made it."

"You made it?" He arched a bushy, white eyebrow at me. "And we're *eating* it?"

"I know. Shocking, isn't it?" I followed him into the kitchen as he set the pot on his stove. "I did cheat a little with pre-cooked chicken, but it looks and smells good if I say so myself."

Grandpa lit his burner, lifted the pot lid, and inhaled. "Yummy. What spices did you use?"

"No idea!" I laughed. "When Darnell cooked for us, he left a bag of spices in my cabinet so I threw that in. So, you're a guinea pig."

"I'm all in," Grandpa said. "If my granddaughtah made it, then I'm trying it."

"What boys are we entertaining tonight?" I pushed a chair over and plucked two highball glasses from an overhead shelf.

"Since you cooked, we need to celebrate," he replied. "There's a bottle of Glenfiddich 21 in the back of the liquor cabinet."

"Ooh the good stuff," I exclaimed. "That's even better than Johnnie Walker Blue."

"Only the best for my granddaughtah." He smiled wide at me.

As I served us the chicken lo mein, Grandpa poured us three fingers full of whiskey.

He clinked his glass against mine. "Here's to your first cooked meal."

"Thank you."

Grandpa forked a bite into his mouth. "This is wicked good. Compliments to the chef."

"Thanks. It called for green onions but I didn't have any. I hope it's still okay?"

"I don't like 'em anyway," Grandpa said. "Or rathah, they don't like me." He tenderly rubbed his stomach.

"Good." I took a bite and surprised myself with my culinary skills. "I didn't have any chicken broth either so I Googled a substitute and it said to use white wine."

"That's my kind of replacement!" Grandpa ate another forkful.

265

"Maybe next weekend I'll tackle your chowder."

"We'll make it togethah," he replied. "I might even let you in on my secret ingredient." He winked at me.

After we finished dinner, we sipped our whiskey at the kitchen table.

"I've been meaning to ask you," Grandpa said. "Did you ever get your birthday present from me?"

"I don't think so."

"I ordahed something from your Amazon gift list."

Oh no. More after-effects from riding the Ambien walrus a month ago.

"What did you get me?"

"A subscription to *Cranes Today* magazine," he replied. He pulled his glasses from his nose, cleaned them with the edge of his shirt, and placed them back on his face. "I thought it was strange but since you specifically requested it, I figahed you had a reason."

"I did." I slapped a hand to my forehead.

I told Grandpa the story of my drugged-up night. Hopefully, the magazine subscription was the last of the strange gifts.

266

CHAPTER 33

The next morning, I strolled into work and found Jenna at her desk.

"Mornin' sunshine," she said with a broad smile.

"You too." I gestured to her all blonde hair. "The pink is gone."

Jenna twirled a golden strand in her fingers. "Yeah, I figured it was time to look my age."

"I always referred to you as my friend with the pink strand. What brought this on? You buying mom jeans without holes too?" I teased.

"Let's not get too crazy," she laughed. "I'll wear them until they fall apart."

"How are things with Mateo?" I asked, resting my elbows on her high desk.

"Amazing!" A hint of crimson blossomed on Jenna's face. "We were in Newport yesterday walking along the Cliff Walk and a random wave came up and splashed me. Mateo took off his jacket and wrapped it around me so that I wouldn't get chilly. No one has done something like that for me since I left Charleston."

"That's sweet."

"He is." Jenna held the back of her hand to a rosy cheek. "It's only been a short while since we met, but I feel like I've known him my whole life. We talk about everything. It's so easy with him."

"I'm so happy for you." A speck of jealousy fluttered inside me. Not because Jenna now dated my former Friends with Benefits, but because she was in a real relationship with someone and I was alone.

I wanted her happiness. I wanted to settle down. I wanted someone to put his jacket over my shoulders.

I left Jenna and headed to my desk. My boss had left a thick folder, full of a new project for me. That would keep me busy most of the day.

Inside, the hostess in a black and white uniform acknowledged us with a smile. A Tiffany lamp hung overhead, casting soft lighting in the space. "Good afternoon. Two for lunch?" she asked.

"Yes, please," Ebony answered for us.

"Would you like to sit outside in the Roman Garden?"

"Sounds good," Ebony replied.

Ebony and I followed the hostess outside where several tables with red and white umbrellas were nestled inside a terra cotta garden surrounded by tall, green arborvitae. Weekday patrons wearing suits and dresses filled some of the tables, dining on salads and sipping iced coffee.

The hostess showed us an empty table in the corner of the patio and set menus at the place settings. "David will be your server today. He'll be by to take your orders." And she was off.

Before I perused the menu, I glanced around the Roman Garden. I smirked and Ebony caught me.

"What's that about?" she asked, glaring at me over the top of her open menu. She leaned forward and her long, black braids dangled against the table.

"You know me too well." I smirked again. "The last time I was here, I met Darnell. He was a chef here."

"You gotta let that go."

"I know," I moaned. I hated when Ebony was right. But she was the smartest person I knew, so it was dumb of me not to follow her advice.

I continued, "I am. He texted me three times last week and I deleted them all without replying."

"Good girl."

Before I could respond, David approached our table wearing a white tuxedo shirt, a black bowtie, a black vest, and matching black trousers. His dark hair was trimmed short.

"Good afternoon ladies," he said. "What can I bring you to drink today?"

"Can I get a chardonnay?" Ebony answered.

"Day-drinking, I see," I whispered to her with a sly grin.

"Get one too," she suggested. "My treat."

"One for me too, please," I told David.

"Perfect," he said. "Would you like any appetizers? Oysters on the half shell or Baccala perhaps?"

"If I ate that and a regular lunch, I wouldn't eat for a week," I joked. "Just an antipasto salad for me, please."

"I'll take a pickled beet salad," Ebony spoke.

"Great choices," David replied, without writing anything down. "I'll be back with your drinks." He collected our menus and he was off.

"Tell me more about Luke's momma," Ebony prodded.

"She's your typical Rhode Island mother," I began. "Very proud of her son and thinks he walks on water."

"Fitting that he's a boat wrapper, huh?"

"Yep. She won't venture out of her eating comfort zone either. If you offer her something new, like gator bites, she'll continually ask you 'Are you sure?'. She won't start a conversation with you so you have to start it. She's had the same friends since elementary school because they all still live in the same area and that's all they know. They don't branch out. If you want her to like you, ask her questions about herself."

"Easy. I do that all the time with my clients." Ebony waved a loose hand into the air.

"It doesn't hurt to bring her flowers either," I added.

"I was planning on it anyway."

"She likes pink roses," I said. "Plus be aware that she still might try to set up Luke with a daughter of her neighbor or a friend. She might even do it in front of you. It's no disrespect to you. That's how I met him. That's how everyone's mom is around here. It's who they are."

"Good to know." Ebony nodded.

A minute later, David came back with our wine.

I held my glass up toward Ebony. "Here's to you making a good impression on Luke's mom."

"Thanks." She clinked her glass against mine.

My phone rang from inside my bag, interrupting us.

"Do you mind if I get that?" I asked Ebony. "It might be work."

"Go ahead." She flicked her fingers at me.

I rummaged through my bag and pulled out my phone. As I read the caller ID, my jaw fell open into an O.

"Holy crap," I muttered.

"Who is it?" Ebony wanted to know.

"Darnell."

CHAPTER 34

"Answer it!" Ebony shrieked.

"But what if--" I started to say. The phone rang again in my hand.

"Answer it," Ebony spoke quickly so as not to let Darnell go to my voicemail. "Find out what he wants."

"You're right." I tapped my phone on and held it to my ear. "Hello?"

"Reese, you okay?" Darnell asked. Concern dripped in his voice.

"Yeah, why?" I replied and shrugged to Ebony.

"Didn't know if you got my texts and wanted to make sure everything's okay."

"I'm good."

"Okay cool. I hadn't heard from you and wondered."

"Like I said, I'm fine." Darnell had a lot of interest in me for someone who had a girlfriend.

"Okay good," he said. "Do you have plans tomorrow night?"

"I don't think so. Why?"

Ebony scrunched her nose at me, trying to figure out Darnell's side of the conversation.

Darnell spoke, "You wanna have dinner with me? I'll cook up something good for us."

"Um, won't your girlfriend mind?" My voice rose to a snarky level.

"Girlfriend? What girlfriend?"

"The one at the docks the other morning."

"Zoe?"

Zoe. That was her name. It was good to finally put a name to her face.

"Yeah, Zoe."

"She's not my girlfriend," Darnell explained.

"Then why did she call you *babe*?"

Darnell laughed out loud. "She calls everyone *babe*. The boat skipper. Everyone on my staff. Our customers. Even the mailman."

Part of me wanted to laugh with him. The other part of me had every reason to believe that he and Zoe were a couple. Couples called each other *babe* all the time. It went with the territory.

"If you say so." I rolled my eyes even though Darnell couldn't see me.

"It's true," Darnell replied. "I wouldn't have a chance with her anyway. Because… she asked me about *you*."

"What?" I blinked, trying to process what I just heard.

"Zoe's into girls."

I laughed so hard I almost knocked my wine glass over.

"What? What did he say?" Ebony asked, and I waved her off.

I smiled wide and mouthed to her, "I'll tell you later."

Darnell spoke again, "Now that you believe me that I'm not dating Zoe, do you want you to have dinner with me?"

277

Everything I've wanted in the past few weeks was finally in front of me.

"Yes," I said, still chuckling. "I'd love that."

"My place. Tomorrow at six."

"See you then."

I hung up with Darnell and Ebony glared at me.

"Well?" Her brown eyes bore into me. "What was that about?"

"Turns out the girl at the dock--Zoe--is not his girlfriend," I said. My face flushed.

"Well, yeah, I figured that out when you said, 'then why did she call you babe.'"

I laughed again, still finding humor in the unexpected twist. "Darnell said that Zoe's into girls and that she was interested in *me*."

Ebony chuckled with me and took a sip of her wine. "That's funny. I didn't see that one coming at all."

"Me either. And Darnell asked me to come over for dinner tomorrow night," I said.

"You're joking?" Ebony stopped midair trying to set her wine glass back on the table.

"Nope."

"I didn't see that one coming either. You okay with it?"

278

"Yeah. Now that I know that he's single, it's all good." I smiled, content with the unexpected turn of events. I could have kicked myself for ignoring Darnell's texts had I known sooner he was single. My stupid jumping to conclusions. Thinking back, even though Zoe called him babe, he didn't reciprocate. That should have been my first clue.

David came back to our table and presented our salads.

"Anything else I can get for you ladies?" he asked.

"No, I think we're good," I spoke for both of us.

"Good. Enjoy your meal. I'll be back to check on you later." David left us with our lunch.

"What's Darnell cooking for you?" Ebony asked, taking a forkful of beets and kale.

"No idea. He said he'll make something good."

"Anything that man makes is always *fine*," Ebony joked with a cunning grin. "Just like him."

"Hey! What about Luke?"

"I'm not dead!"

"But seriously, do you think he's into me now?" I inhaled deeply, nervous about my question.

279

"I would hope so," Ebony replied. "He asked you to come over for dinner."

"But what will I say to him? What if he's simply being himself and I miss the signs again?"

"Just tell him how you feel. If he doesn't say the same, then you'll know. You have to take the leap. Besides, if I hear any more about you whining over Darnell, I might have to beat you with a stick."

I chuckled at Ebony's casual threat. "You're right. You're always right." The Queen of Queens reigned again.

"I know." Ebony winked at me. "That's why we're best friends."

CHAPTER 35

After work the next day, I paced my kitchen like a caged animal. In an hour, I would be having dinner with Darnell--something I've wanted for a while. I was thrilled he was single. But at the same time, so many of my questions still needed answers. He helped me cook for my grandpa and didn't mind standing shirtless in my house. (Oh, his amazing body.) But when I visited him at his food truck, he walked off when I couldn't explain about Luke and Mateo. What was running through his head? How did he feel about me? What was his end game? Or did he have no plan after tonight?

For as long as I had known Darnell, he wasn't one to play games. But he was killin' me. When we dated, I never got the impression that he was hiding something or skulking in a corner with a leggy brunette. He was there for me when I needed a last-minute date for a work dinner at the governor's mansion. He said what was on his mind and everything was easy with him. As busy as he was at work, I could always count on him to call me when he was on his way home. He never complained when I brought documents home to review and interrupted our dinner.

He was sweet, kind, thoughtful, and put others before himself. I still kicked myself for letting him go. I was such a fool.

But now I had the chance to redeem myself. I only hoped he felt the same way.

My heart ratcheted inside my chest like a jackhammer. The sensation was so strong I could barely feel my clothes against my skin. If a doctor put a stethoscope to my chest, she'd probably order an EKG. My face warmed and my breathing intensified. I needed to chill because, if Darnell saw me like this, I couldn't utter a coherent phrase.

I needed to calm down. And fast. I ran over to my liquor cabinet and scanned the contents. Red wine. Jameson. Whipped vodka. Ehh. None of that was a good idea because I didn't want to be drunk in front of Darnell. Back in the kitchen, I rummaged through the drawers searching for a solution. Take out menus. Rubber bands. Pens. There it was. The solution to help calm my nerves. The single packet of Japanese tea from my cousin Julia. Who would've thought that an inadvertent birthday wish list present would be a welcomed solution?

My hand trembled as I filled a coffee cup with water and nearly spilling it when I put it in the microwave. I couldn't remember the last time I was this nervous about a guy. Until recently, I had a carefree lifestyle and didn't apologize for it. But to have this second chance with Darnell would change everything. If he would have me, I'd immediately deactivate my Tinder account, hang up my single-girl hat, and decline any dates Mrs. Patterson would try to set me up on. I had zero interest in other men. I only wanted Darnell.

When my water was hot, I slipped the tea bag into the cup, letting the water permeate the dried herbs. While the tea steeped, I laid a hand to my chest and my heart thumped against my fingers. Talking to Darnell could calm my nerves, even though I had no idea if his feelings were the same as mine. He was what I needed.

I only hoped he felt the same. Telling him everything terrified me because I was so afraid of what he might say.

I sipped the hot tea in two hands, careful not to burn my tongue. The toasty and nutty flavors filled me with warmth, giving me psychosomatic confidence that everything would be okay. Even if Darnell didn't reciprocate, I would at least have an answer and could move on.

After I finished the tea, I ran upstairs with a burst of energy and headed toward my closet. I pulled out my favorite blue and pink wrap dress and slipped it on. In the bathroom armed with a flat iron and an arsenal of makeup, I added some waves to my otherwise straight blonde hair and dotted my lashes with mascara and eyeliner. I slid into flat sandals and did one final primp in front of the mirror. Eat your heart out, Darnell, because I'm coming.

With a bottle of wine in my hand, I was out the door.

Darnell lived on Harkness Street on the west side of Federal Hill, in the heart of the gourmand neighborhood. He told me he purchased his condo when he worked at Camille's because he could walk to work.

Fifteen minutes later, I pulled up in front of the century-old red clapboard-siding house where Darnell lived on the second floor. I could see the edge of his vegetable garden around the back end of the property. With the bottle of wine and my phone in my hands, I walked to his door. My heart rapped as if a woodpecker lived in my chest. Apparently, the calming effects of the tea had worn off. What was I doing? I hesitated on the porch, hand in mid-air before ringing Darnell's doorbell. I wanted to turn around, drive back home, and crawl under my covers. That was the easiest thing to do. But he was the love of my life. I had to tell him. Damn the answer.

Taking a deep breath, I closed my eyes, rang the doorbell, and hoped for the best. Maybe this time the relationship gods would be on my side.

When I opened my eyes, Darnell stood in front of me through his screen door. My heart instantly slowed at the sight of him in a navy-blue button-down shirt and dark jeans. Damn, he looked good.

"Hi, Reese." He opened the screen door and kissed me on the cheek. Wow, he smelled good - like hazelnuts and vanilla, as if he knew that the scents would calm me. "You look amazing."

I blushed.

"Thanks. I brought this." I held up the wine.

"Perfect." He grinned. "Come on in." He led me up the interior steps to his living space. I hadn't been inside in almost two years, but everything was as I remembered. His brown leather couch nestled comfortably under a stained-glass window. We spent many a night there watching movies and laughing at reruns of *Mystery Science Theater*. A painting of famed chef Leah Chase, Queen of Creole Cuisine, hung on the side wall. Small pots of herbs cluttered his windowsills.

He led me into his kitchen. His perfect gourmet kitchen. We stopped at his island and I placed the bottle of wine on it, next to a bowl of lemons and limes. On the wall next to me was a three-row rack of dozens of spices. I could read the names but had no idea how they were used. Maybe Darnell could teach me one day? I would gladly be his assistant. A crock full of cooking utensils rested on the kitchen counter. Next to it was a turbo-charged mixer. I envied his cooking prowess.

"You'll never guess what I made the other day." I put my phone on the island and leaned on my elbows, making myself comfortable as much as possible, hoping to force out my nerves.

"A piece of toast?" Darnell joked. His broad smile filled his face.

"Touché," I tsked. "No. Chicken lo mein for dinner with my grandpa."

Darnell arched an eyebrow at me. "Chicken lo mein? For real? That's a five-step recipe."

"Actually, it's three," I corrected him. "And I used your leftover spices."

"Nobody helped you?" Darnell asked as he pulled a couple of wine glasses and a corkscrew from his overhead cabinet.

"Nope." I grinned, proud of my accomplishment. "Why? Would you be jealous if someone had?"

"Maybe." He opened the wine bottle, poured it into the glasses, and handed one to me. "Us chefs like to know our competition."

Did he mean that professionally? Or personally? I liked that he could still make me wonder about him.

Darnell raised his glass. "To you. For making your first dish by yourself."

"Thank you." I clinked my glass against his and we both took a sip.

287

"How did your grandpa like it anyway?"

"He loved it. He even pulled out a bottle of Glenfiddich 21 to celebrate the occasion."

Darnell blew out a low whistle. "That's the good stuff."

"I know. He doesn't bring that out for just anything." Chatting with Darnell was effortless. I almost forgot how nervous I was earlier. But I needed to take my time to tell him how I felt about him. Maybe after dinner.

"Are you hungry?" he asked as if he read my mind.

"Always."

"I have some harissa salmon and potatoes in the oven and I pulled some arugula from my garden for a salad," Darnell said and turned toward his oven. "Had I known you were now a chef, I would have waited and had you help me make it."

"That sounds pretty complicated." I nervously gulped some wine at the thought. "I can't get too cocky. Don't want to burn down your house."

"Don't worry." Darnell faced me again. "I'd be gentle."

I swallowed hard. Did he mean what I think he meant?

Darnell spoke again, "Don't want to scare you off from cooking again."

Of course. Mental head slap.

"I'd still like to help. Can I set the table?" I asked.

"Sure." Darnell nodded toward an upper cabinet to the right of the sink. "The plates are in there."

"I remember," I said with a grin.

I grabbed two plates from the cabinet, two sets of utensils from the drawer below, and carried them to the dining room. White cloth napkins were already on the table. On a second trip, I brought our wine glasses and the rest of the bottle.

When I came back to the kitchen, Darnell was unloading the salmon and potatoes from the oven.

"That looks great," I said. The salmon was a perfect pink and the potatoes had puckered in all the right places. Something that I could never achieve. "Compliments to the chef."

"Thank you." He decanted the fish and potatoes onto a serving tray. "I hope you like it."

I liked anything that Darnell would give me.

"Can you grab the salad from the fridge?" he asked.

"Sure."

We carried the food to the dining room, set it on the table, and sat down.

"I'm glad you came tonight," Darnell said, as he served me a plateful.

"Me too. I'm sorry I ignored your texts." I unfolded a cloth napkin on my lap.

"I was starting to think you were ghosting me." Darnell served himself a plate.

"It was a big misunderstanding. I'm sorry." I forked some salmon into my mouth. "Wow, this is amazing."

"Thank you. It's a new recipe. I'm glad you like it." Darnell took a bite as well.

We spent the next half hour laughing, talking, drinking, and eating. A few times he grazed my arm with his fingers and lingered on my forehead with a kiss. I couldn't remember the last time I had this much fun on a date. My body warmed with the thought of telling Darnell how I felt about him.

CHAPTER 36

With an empty plate and full stomach, I swallowed the last drop of wine from my glass. Garnering as much liquid courage as I could, I spoke. "Darnell, I want to talk to you about something."

He cocked his head to the side and stared at me. His brown eyes glistened. "What about?"

"I don't even know where to begin, so I'm gonna say it." How I wished for more wine to help me talk.

"Is it something I did?" Darnell rested his hand on the table, a few inches from mine. Was he trying to touch me or was it my imagination getting the best of me again?

"No, no. That's not it. You're fine. You're more than fine. You're perfect."

Darnell stared at me, unblinking.

I broke his gaze and glanced out the dining room window for a moment. The September sun was starting to set and the sky was filled with pink and yellow hues.

"Reese, what're you getting at?" he asked. "I'm far from perfect."

I loved his modesty. Another amazing thing about him.

I took a deep breath and spoke again. "I mean I messed up breaking up with you and I regret it every day. I love spending time with you. You are responsible for the happiness I didn't know I could feel. You inspire me to reach for things beyond just living day-to-day. Everything is easy with you. I want to be with you again--if you'll have me."

Darnell pulled his hand away from me and pursed his lips. Ouch. Not the response I expected when I just spilled my guts.

"What about those guys I met at your house last month?" he asked. "I don't want to be your second choice. Or third choice." Darnell folded his arms across his chest. "I won't be in some weird version of *The Bachelorette*."

"You're not. Everything is over with both of them. I swear." He was making this hard for me, but I needed to be honest with him if we had any chance of starting fresh.

"You haven't seen either one of them since?"

I chewed my bottom lip. "Well, yes."

"Reese…" Darnell picked up his plate and started to get up from the table.

"It's not like that." I grabbed his arm before he could walk away like he did at his food truck the last time we had this conversation.

"Then what's it like?" Darnell recoiled from my grip. He jerked his arm away from me.

Then it hit me. "Is this why you left me hanging at the dance and your food truck? Even though we seemed to be getting along?"

Darnell nodded. "I was getting a little too comfortable with you and I needed to step back because I didn't want to get hurt again."

"And because you think you were another notch on my bedpost?"

293

Darnell recoiled. "What was I supposed to think when I met those guys at your house? It's pretty obvious you have an entourage."

"Yes. I do. I mean I did," I sputtered. "I realized I don't want to date either one of them anymore. Or anyone else." Even though both Mateo and Luke were now dating my friends, I would have ended things for good with them anyway. I wanted Darnell. Only Darnell. "I only want to date you. If you'll have me." I begged him with pleading eyes.

His brown gaze bore into me. He was the most beautiful man I had ever met. Inside and out.

I spoke again. "I was such an idiot to let you go the first time."

"How do I know you won't break up with me again?" He rubbed a hand along his beard.

I wanted to reassure him that would never happen but he was too pragmatic for that. "I promise you that I want to be with you. And only you. Right here. Right now."

"Keep going," Darnell pushed.

"I was stupid to let you go. I thought I wanted to be independent and not have a care in the world. But being around you this past month has changed all that.

294

You have no idea how jealous I was of Zoe when I first saw her. The fact that she had you--and I didn't--burned me up."

"I told you that she and I weren't together." He sat back down in his chair.

"I know, but the initial thought of you being with someone else and that I had lost my chance with you forever made me miserable." I got up from the table and paced the dining room. "I don't even want to tell you the crazy thought that ran through my head."

Darnell stayed in his seat and watched me.

I continued, "I can't believe I'm telling you all this. I never thought I would." I stopped at the windows and gazed out, purposely not facing Darnell because I was afraid of his reaction. He was being so hard on me. It was killing me.

"Why not?" he asked.

"Because I've been terrified of what you might say." I chewed on my fingernail, still looking out the window. A woman walking her dog strolled down the street. "That you might not care about me the same way I feel about you."

"How do you feel about me?" he asked.

295

I turned and caught his eyes in mine. Those soulful, brown, kind eyes. I could get lost in them. He was the most wonderful man I had ever met. Plus, he had no idea how handsome he was. And the rest of his body. Wow. His biceps formed toned mounds under his navy-blue shirt. If I ever had the chance to run my hands along his abs again, I would melt into a pile of mush. He was the perfect package. He had everything I never knew I wanted. Until now.

"You are the greatest love of my life. I love you." I spoke barely above a whisper, my heart thumping in a cacophony of nerves. I stared at him, frozen, waiting for a response. Any response.

Without a word, Darnell stood up from the table and walked out of the dining room toward the back of the condo.

Oh no, not again.

I dropped my head in defeat and my eyes swelled with tears. I couldn't believe he left me. And without an explanation or even an, 'I'm sorry I don't feel the same way.' I was so stupid. Again. I had to get out of there before he came back and I felt like an even bigger idiot.

296

I rushed out of the dining room and down the stairs as fast as my short legs could take me. Being vertically challenged did not help in moments like this. At the bottom, I fought with the front door to open, jiggling the doorknob in my hands--stupid old New England houses--and ran to my car. That's when the dam broke. Tears gushed down my cheeks, blocking my vision. I stopped on the sidewalk near the Impala and hunched over, letting all of the emotions drain out of me. Through coughs and hiccups, more tears flowed. I used the hem of my dress to wipe my face, not caring if I flashed anyone. More tears came.

What a selfish jerk I was. I mistakenly convinced myself that I could be with Darnell again. He had every right to turn me down. He was an amazing guy, but he couldn't trust me not to hurt him again. He set me up by asking me how I felt about him only to have him walk off and leave me all alone. He had every right to do that.

I stood upright and wiped my face with the back of my hand. Errant smears of mascara and eyeliner streaked my hand. Damn. Now I looked like a football player who sweated off his eye black.

In my haste to get out the door, I left my phone on Darnell's kitchen island. At least my keys were in the

297

pocket of my dress. I could still drive away and put some space between us. My phone could wait. I tried to unlock my car, but the old Impala decided to be stubborn and not let me in. The sound of footsteps caught my attention.

"Reese!" Darnell ran up to me, out of breath. His dark eyes bore into me. "Don't go. I came back into the dining room and you were gone! I heard you running out. Why'd you leave?"

I faced him, planting my hands on my hips. "Because when I told you I loved you, you left me. Obviously, you don't care about me so I assumed you were saying no."

"I didn't say anything," Darnell corrected me. "That wasn't a *no*."

"It wasn't a *yes,* either," I muttered.

"I got up because I wanted to get you this." Darnell reached into his pants pocket and pulled out a small light blue box.

"An engagement ring?" I wondered out loud. "Don't you think--"

Darnell chuckled. "No. Don't get ahead of yourself. Just open it." He held it to me.

I opened the lid and found a sterling silver bar necklace. Three small diamonds illuminated the middle of it.

"What's this for?" I asked, gazing back at Darnell. "I was a total mess back inside."

"For your 30th birthday," he replied. "I was waiting for the right moment to give it to you. It's the right moment."

"Oh my god," I whispered. Stunned, I cupped a hand to my mouth. Running out of Darnell's condo like a crazy person fell to the wayside. "Thank you. It's beautiful. I can't believe you did this. I love it."

"I wanted to give you something special. Because you helped me. Here, let me put it on you."

Darnell tugged the necklace out of the box. As I held up my hair, he linked it around my neck.

"How did I help you?" I let my hair fall back down.

"If it wasn't for you, I never would have opened my food truck," he explained. Darnell grasped my hand in his. The instant warmth filled me to my core. "And I wanted to thank you for it."

"What do you mean if it wasn't for me?" I questioned. "I didn't even know you had a food truck until last month." I didn't want to let go of his hand. Being connected to him calmed me.

"When we dated, you made me believe I could change my life." Darnell wiped a stray tear from my face with his free hand. "You charmed me that first night I met you. It sounds silly, but I think I was meant to undercook that steak. Otherwise, I never would have met you."

"What did I do?"

"You taught me to believe in myself," Darnell said. A warm smile formed on his mouth. "Every time I had a pipe dream, you gave me ideas on how to achieve it. Even as simple as telling me to cut my cable to save some money for the truck. You always encouraged me to be better. To do better. To believe in myself. I am always blown away by you. I wouldn't be where I am without you. You were the inspiration for my tattoo."

That Latin script tattoo on his gorgeous, smooth chest.

Words struggled to form in my mouth.

Darnell continued, "I wanted you to know how much of an impact you've had on my life."

He let go of my hand, turned to face me, and held both of my shoulders in his hands. "Reese, I love you. I've always loved you. I haven't dated anyone since you broke up with me. I had always hoped deep down you might change your mind about me. What we had was amazing."

"Then why did you give me a hard time upstairs? Letting me go on and on without saying anything." I took a step back, without breaking his hold.

"Because I wanted to be sure you were being legit. I couldn't let you break my heart again. I couldn't go through that again. It hurt too much the first time."

"I'm so sorry," I sniffed. "I never want to break your heart again."

"Reese, you are one of the strongest people I know. I am blessed to have you in my life. Even though we might not have talked all the time, the time we spent together will never be taken away from us. When we talk now, it's like time stood still. I can't explain it - like a time warp where those two years apart faded away."

Darnell curved his fingers around my chin. He kissed me and my body instantly burned, as if we could melt a hole in the earth together.

Darnell broke the kiss and spoke. "I want you all the time. Why do you think I texted you like I did?"

"I'm glad you did." A fluttering filled my stomach. "You are so amazing. I am so happy."

"I have a tiny confession to make." Darnell's lip curled upward into a sly grin.

"What?" I couldn't imagine what he had been keeping from me.

"Do you remember my Great-Aunt Chandra?"

"How could I forget? She tried to set us up at the dance," I chuckled.

"In more ways than one," Darnell added. He slid a strong arm around my waist and pulled me close to him. Wow, he smelled good.

"What do you mean by that?"

"Turns out she and your grandpa were conspiring to get us back together all along."

"What?" I broke his hold and glared at him.

"I guess you told him one night how you felt about me?" Darnell grinned at me as if he was spilling a big secret.

"Yeah, I guess I did. I totally forgot."

"Then your grandpa told my great-aunt when she had some of your grandpa's chowder and then she told me."

"Those stinkers! You big jerk!" I laughed out loud and swatted Darnell in the arm. "You knew all along how I felt about you and you let me go and on without saying a word. I was such a nervous freak upstairs!"

"I got what I wanted, didn't I?" Darnell grinned again and planted another kiss on me.

CHAPTER 37

A few days later, Darnell and I fluttered around my kitchen. We had just returned from Shaw's with several bags of groceries to replenish my desolate fridge. I unpacked as he found new homes for everything. I would never be the master chef that he was. Darnell was on a mission to teach me to cook--and other things--without burning down the house.

The necklace around my neck hadn't moved since Darnell put it there.

"Do you want to make shrimp scampi or stuffed meatballs?" He held shrimp in one hand and a pound of ground beef in the other.

"Shrimp scampi is delicious, but it sounds scary to make," I gulped.

Darnell finished loading my fridge and pulled me into his arms. "Don't worry, I got you."

"I know you do." I kissed him. Those warm lips sent tingles down to my toes.

After we put the rest of the groceries away, I grabbed a frying pan from a lower cabinet and put it on the stove. Darnell sliced off a pat of butter and set it on the counter. He had also laid out chopped garlic, salt, crushed red pepper, black pepper, a lemon, and the thawed shrimp. I had grabbed a bottle of white wine from my fridge.

He stood behind me, his hot breath sending chills down my spine. "Take the butter and slide it into the hot pan, let it melt until it's smooth and a little bubbly."

I did as instructed, feeling Darnell's body heat against my back. The kitchen was getting warm in more ways than one.

"Now add the garlic and let it cook for a minute," he said.

As I did, my kitchen filled with the distinguished aroma.

"The wine is next," Darnell instructed as he leaned into me. Mmm. He smelled so good.

"How much do I pour?" I asked, still dumbfounded that he could cook without measuring.

"I'll let you know when to stop."

I opened the bottle, tilted it over the pan, and a stream of golden liquid poured out.

"Keep going," Darnell said. "You need a good half cup."

I let the wine fill an inch of the pan.

"Okay, that's plenty. Next, add a good shake of salt and pepper, but only a tap of red pepper flakes. Unless you want it hot."

"It's plenty hot in here," I bantered.

"Let's let it cook for two minutes so it will reduce by half."

"Aren't we setting a timer?" I asked.

"No. I'm kissing you for two minutes and that'll be enough."

"I'm down with that."

Darnell turned me to face him and leaned into me. I tilted my head upwards, opening my mouth. Darnell's tongue intertwined around mine, intoxicating me. Moaning into him, my mind lost all thoughts as my body felt like it was on fire. I couldn't wait to do more naughty things with him.

After a few hot moments, Darnell released me. "There. Your wine is ready."

"Wow," I whispered. "We'll have to set a timer like that more often."

"Mmm hmm." Darnell sighed. "You ready for the next step?"

"If it involves kissing you more, then yes."

"Add in the shrimp in a single layer," he instructed. "Let it cook a couple of minutes until it turns pink on the bottom."

"How will I know if it's pink if I can't see the bottom?" I asked the novice question.

"The edges will turn a little pink and the top will get opaque." Darnell handed me a small spatula out of my barely opened tool drawer. "Then turn them over and cook the other side."

"Gotcha."

While I flipped the shrimp, Darnell cut the lemon in half and handed it to me. "Squeeze this over top."

I squirted the fresh lemon juice all over the shrimp. The citrus scent permeated my nose. "Oh, that smells good."

"Like the flavor of the gods."

He leaned into me, his warm body encircling mine. There was more heat between us than on the stove. He kissed me hard and ran his hand along my back, pulling me even closer to him. I loved his musky scent.

"What's next?" I breathed out.

"That's it," Darnell whispered. "Unless you want a side of angel hair or something?"

"Nah, I'm good with this. One thing at a time. Don't want to get too cocky." I separated myself from him just long enough to turn off the stove.

Darnell cackled at my self-deprecation.

"But that was easy." I felt so proud of myself.

"Anyone can cook--"

"--with a cute teacher like you," I completed his sentence. I winked at him.

We filled two plates with my masterpiece and settled at the kitchen table.

"I have a dumb question," Darnell said as he took a forkful of shrimp. "What's with the big block of cheese in your fridge?"

I laughed out loud. "The short-short answer is that my Uncle Charlie sent it for my birthday."

"That's kind of a weird present, but okay," Darnell smirked. "What's the long answer?"

Slapping a hand to my face, I shook my head and chuckled again. That's right, I had never told Darnell about my wild adventures riding the Ambien walrus.

I relayed the story of how I blacked out, texted him, Mateo, and Luke, and managed to fill out a birthday wish list from Amazon resulting in odd gifts from my relatives and old friends.

"You added cheese to your gift list," Darnell smirked. "Now that's funny."

"I'm really not sure. I never checked it and my Uncle Charlie is a little whacky anyway."

"We all have eccentric family members," Darnell agreed.

"But what am I supposed to do with twelve pounds of cheese?" I asked. "I hate for it to go to waste. No way am I eating it."

"I think I have an idea." Darnell scratched his beard.

* * * *

After dinner, Darnell and I walked out back to check out my garden. The September sun was starting to set, casting an orange glow on my plants.

"I haven't been out here in almost a week," I confessed. "The local critters might have gotten to it, so I don't know what's left."

Darnell leaned down and plucked a few late-blooming tomatoes from the plants. "These are good. We can make a salad with them tomorrow."

"Good idea." I liked the fact that Darnell was making plans with me - even if it was only for the next day. I was happy and in love with an amazing man.

Mrs. Patterson waddled out of her house and waved to us from the other side of the hedge. "How you doing tonight, deeyah?"

"Fine, Mrs. Patterson. How are you?"

"My back hurts again, but the good Lahd hasn't taken me, so I can't complain." She looked quizzically at Darnell picking my tomatoes. "Who's that with you?"

"Darnell." He stood up and I squeezed his hand in mine.

"Good to meet you, Dahnell," she said. "Reese is a good girl. You take care of her." She waved a crooked finger at him.

"Yes, ma'am," Darnell replied with a grin. "I plan on it."

Mrs. Patterson tilted her head as if the mouse on the wheel started running again. "You two will make beautiful babies."

Darnell and I laughed out loud and said goodnight to Mrs. Patterson. We headed inside as he carried an armful of tomatoes.

Once in the house, Darnell set the freshly picked produce on my kitchen counter.

"I can't believe Mrs. Patterson said that about making babies," I giggled and jumped up on the counter next to him.

"Maybe we don't want babies yet, but we could practice *making* them..."

Darnell moved in front of me, slid his body between my knees, and hoisted me off of the counter. He skimmed his mouth along my neck, scratching me with his beard.

"You're the sexiest woman I've ever known," he whispered in my ear. "I love how easily you turn me on."

I wrapped my legs around him and he carried me up the stairs to my bedroom.

CHAPTER 38

On the last Saturday of September, Darnell's food truck was parked near the edge of the basketball courts at Billy Taylor Park. Neighborhood kids and their parents gathered in the green space. Some sprawled out on blankets on the grass, some shot hoops, while others ran around giggling and playing tag. The sun shone down on the late summer day, bringing a slight breeze in the air.

Sporting *Farmfood* t-shirts, Darnell and I and the rest of his staff crammed inside the truck preparing sandwiches. Grilled cheese sandwiches. When I burned a few, I was relegated to serving. So much for my cooking confidence.

A couple of weeks earlier, Darnell asked one of his vendors to donate bread and I supplied the cheese for a Mt. Hope Grilled Cheese Fest. Shaw's donated bottled water and Stop & Shop contributed ice cream bars. The proceeds would go toward new playground equipment at the park. Darnell told his kids at the community garden to spread the word and now the place was packed with grateful afternoon diners. I recognized several of them at the park.

With trays full of sandwiches, Darnell and I jumped out of the truck and distributed them to everyone. As we passed them out to hungry kids and parents, Zoe approached us from the parking lot.

"Sorry I'm late." Shiny new garden tools filled her arms. "I was waiting on the park board president to get these to me."

"That's great," Darnell quipped. "Just set them on the other side of the truck. We'll put them inside at the end of the day and take them with us. I'll surprise the kids with them on Wednesday."

"Do we know who the donor was?" Zoe asked.

"No, the person wanted to remain anonymous," Darnell answered.

"I think I might know," I interrupted them. I almost forgot about the check I wrote a month earlier.

"You do?" Darnell and Zoe said in unison.

"It was when I wasn't sure if you would talk to me again." I pointed to Darnell. "I wanted to thank you for cooking for my grandpa."

"What a wicked gift. That was generous of you, babe," Zoe said to me. She carried the tools to the backside of the food truck.

When she was out of sight, I laughed at her moniker for me.

"I told you," Darnell talked out of the side of his mouth.

God, he was hot. And sweet.

After I handed off my last sandwich, I headed back to the truck to replenish my supply. Zoe came around the corner of the truck and stopped me.

"I remember you from the dock a few weeks ago," she said.

"Yeah, that was me."

She closed the personal space between us and ran a finger along my forearm. "You're cute. If you ever want to come play for the other team, let me know."

314

I choked down a nervous laugh and almost dropped my tray.

"I'm good. Thanks," I replied. "If I ever change my mind, you'll be the first one I call."

"I promise you I'll make it worth your while," she whispered in my ear.

My mouth fell open. Before I could respond, she stepped away and climbed inside the truck. I guessed Darnell wasn't kidding about that either.

"Reese!" Several female voices caught my attention.

I faced up as Ebony, Val, and Jenna came toward me. Luke, Mateo, and Aidan followed a few steps behind the girls. Val and Aidan's dog, Charlotte, trailed next to them on a leash. They pulled me into a group hug.

"This is awesome," Ebony spoke first. "You have a huge crowd."

"Thanks," I said with a smile. "But all I did was contribute the cheese."

"How's everything with Darnell?" Jenna said.

"Great." I nodded behind her. "Ask him yourself." Darnell joined our group and slid a hand around my waist. "Do you remember the girls?"

315

"It's been a while," he said, "but yeah. How you doing?" He extended a hand to Luke, Mateo, and Aidan. "Good to see you guys again. Please help yourself to some sandwiches and drinks. We have plenty, thanks to Reese." He kissed my cheek. I thankful that he was secure seeing his former competition. "She's beautiful, isn't she?"

One of the staff members called Darnell from the truck.

"Sorry, I gotta go. Work calls," he said. "Good to see you again." He waved to us and climbed into the truck.

"You two look good together," Val told me. "I'm happy for you."

"Thanks." I blushed. "Everything's been wonderful with him. I still can't believe we're back together. We see each other almost every day and he's the last person I want to talk to before I go to bed. And last week, I deleted my Tinder account."

"Speaking of being together," Ebony added, "if it wasn't for you, Luke and I would still be single."

With his long strides, Luke reached Ebony in two steps and leaned over her. He parted her braids and planted a kiss on her forehead.

"Thank you, Reese," he said, towering over her. "She's the best thing that's evah happened to me."

"Me too." Ebony grinned. "I even love his shaggy hair."

"How did everything go with Luke's mom?" I asked.

"She loves Ebony!" he spoke for her. "Said Ebony's the best thing for me."

"I taught her how to drink Buffalo Trace and I'm taking her out for lunch next weekend," Ebony replied. "We're going for Southern Creole."

"Really?" I arched an eyebrow at her. "How did you get her out of her comfort zone?"

"It's Ebony's chahm." Luke pulled her into a bear hug and she kissed him. "Everything I love about this woman. She's wicked smaht and totally hot."

Ebony blushed.

I nodded to Jenna. "How's everything with you two?"

"Amazing," she gushed. She swayed a little in place as if she was dancing to her own tune.

Mateo spoke, "We're making plans to go to Portugal in the spring. We searched for flights this morning." He slipped an arm around Jenna's waist.

317

"I can't wait!" Jenna giggled and kissed him on the cheek.

"That's great." I hugged both of them.

"And we have some news too," Val added. "Now that we're all together, I wanted to tell you."

She and Aidan exchanged sly glances. They wore matching white Vineyard Vines long sleeve t-shirts. The big pink whale seemed to smirk at me.

"I'm pregnant!" Val jumped up and down. "Charlotte's going to have a sibling!"

All seven of us enveloped Val into a group hug with kisses of congratulations. I couldn't have a better group of friends.

As my friends chowed down on grilled cheese sandwiches, another familiar face found his way through the crowd as I was serving others. Kids squealed in the nearby purple and green playground.

"Grandpa!" I set my tray of sandwiches down on a nearby picnic table and rushed over to him.

"How's my favorite peanut buttah cup?" He pulled me into a warm hug. He wore a linen button-down shirt, khakis, and loafers.

"I'm so glad you made it."

"I wouldn't miss it," he said. "Glad to be a paht of the community." He waved to a woman behind him in a sky-blue sundress to join us. "Do you remember Chandra? Don't worry, she drove me."

"Yes, of course. Darnell's aunt." I hadn't seen her since the community center dance. I extended my hand to her. Her grey and black cornrows were swept up into a colorful bandana.

"Don't be silly, baby." Chandra flicked a neon green manicured hand at me, dismissing my gesture. "You're family now." She wrapped her arms around me and embraced me, nearly lifting me off of the ground.

Grandpa smiled in approval.

"Are you getting a grilled cheese sandwich?" I asked. "Darnell's making them."

"Of course," Grandpa exclaimed.

"Your chowder would go great with my nephew's sandwiches," Chandra added. "You two should cook together sometime."

"Nah, my chowdah is reserved for classy ladies like you," Grandpa said.

"Good answer." Chandra kissed my grandpa on the mouth, knocking her saucer-sized silver hoop earrings against his face.

Then she motioned to my neck. "That's a beautiful necklace, baby."

"Thank you." I ran my finger along it. "Darnell gave it to me."

"I know." Grandpa winked at me.

How did he know? I hadn't told him.

"Speaking of that," I lowered my voice and took a step closer to them. "I heard you two were conspiring to get Darnell and me back together."

"I keep telling you, Reese," Grandpa smirked. "You can't get anything past your gramps. And your gramps only wants the best for his peanut buttah cup."

# # #

The End

Thank you for reading my book.
If you enjoyed it, won't you please take a moment to
leave me a review at your favorite retailer?
One or two sentences is perfectly fine.

If you find any errors, please contact me at
marywalshwrites@gmail.com
As a thank you, I'll send you an autographed copy of my
short story *Dragon Slayer*.
Thanks!

Mary Walsh

Follow me on Instagram and Facebook:
@marywalshwrites
marywalshwrites.wixsite.com/author
www.goodreads.com/goodreadscommarywalshwrites

Made in the USA
Middletown, DE
03 July 2021